TO CATCH A LIE

British detective fiction with a hook and a twist

JOHN DEAN

THE BOOK FOLKS

Published by The Book Folks

London, 2024

© John Dean

This book is a work of fiction. Names, characters, businesses, organizations, places and events are either the product of the author's imagination or are used fictitiously. Any resemblance to actual persons, living or dead, events or locales is entirely coincidental.

All rights reserved. No part of this publication may be reproduced, stored in retrieval system, copied in any form or by any means, electronic, mechanical, photocopying, recording or otherwise transmitted without written permission from the publisher.

ISBN 978-1-80462-196-7

www.thebookfolks.com

TO CATCH A LIE is the eleventh novel by John Dean to feature DCI Jack Harris. It can be enjoyed as a standalone or as part of the series. Details of the other books are available at the end of this one.

A list of characters can also be found at the back of this book.

Chapter one

The two anglers waded halfway across the fast-flowing North Pennine river and waited patiently for the telltale flash of movement that would give away the presence of a trout in the dancing waters. They had been promising each other a day's fishing for months but the demands of their jobs as police officers had forced them to cancel on several occasions, much to their chagrin as the days and weeks of the season had slipped away.

Now, finally, they had managed to get together. Jack Harris was the local, the one who knew the river. He was a large man, strong-jawed with thick brown hair, the head of divisional CID in the valley. His visitor was one of his few friends. Graham Leckie was slim with dark hair beginning to thin, a plainclothes constable working in intelligence with Greater Manchester Police who had made the journey north that morning. Both men were relishing the break from their work and appreciating the warmth of the late summer morning sun on their backs as they stood midway across the River Lev and waited for the telltale tug on their lines that would herald the first bite of the day.

'I keep meaning to ask,' said Harris after an hour's companionable silence. 'Have there been any developments on your lot's investigation into the anglers who were attacked?'

'CID made a couple of arrests but couldn't get anything to stick so had to let them go. It's very frustrating.'

'Do they still think it's down to the Anti-Fishing Alliance?'

'That's the theory,' said Leckie. 'It would seem that the AFA has stepped things up, including recruiting three or four hardline animal rights agitators over recent weeks, really wild types by the sound of it. They seem to think that attacking fishermen will help them get fishing banned. It's a worrying escalation.'

'It certainly is,' said Harris. He allowed his gaze to roam across the wooded hillsides of his beloved valley. 'Well, hopefully they'll leave our area alone.'

'Don't bank on it. Word is that they are looking to expand their activities beyond Greater Manchester and they're looking for targets.'

'That's all I need,' said Harris.

The inspector lapsed into a gloomy silence for a few moments as he considered the news. Leckie, meanwhile, gestured to a bend in the river further upstream.

'Is it worth moving further along? The fish are clearly not biting here and we might have better luck.' He glanced across to the riverbank where the inspector's dogs, Scoot, a black Labrador, and Archie, a collie, both of them mixed in with guess-the-breed, were looking increasingly bored. 'And it'll give the boys something to do.'

'It's worth a try,' said Harris. 'But we'll have to head downstream. We can't go upstream.'

'Why not? It looks like it might be excellent fishing beyond the bend.'

'It *is* excellent,' said Harris.

'Then why don't we fish it?'

'I'll explain over a brew,' said the inspector.

Both men waded towards the riverbank where they were greeted enthusiastically by the dogs. Harris's mobile rang.

'I told them that I was not to be disturbed,' he said. He took the device out of the breast pocket of his shirt, saw that the caller was his sergeant, Matthew Gallagher, and put the call on speaker so that Leckie could hear.

'Sorry to disturb you on your day off,' said the detective sergeant. 'How are things in the peaceful world of the trout fisherman?'

'Not so peaceful,' said Harris. 'Graham has just been telling me about a couple of fishermen who were attacked in his area and now some damn fool of a detective sergeant seems to have forgotten that I did not want to be disturbed on my day off. What's happened?'

'Nothing,' said Gallagher. 'It's just that I am drawing up the rotas and remembered that you asked for a week off but I can't seem to find the bit of paper with the dates on.'

'The seventh to the fourteenth,' said Harris.

'I'll make sure it's booked in,' said the sergeant. 'Did you say that a couple of anglers had been attacked? Why on earth would anyone do something like that?'

'They're trying to get fishing banned because they say it's cruel,' said Harris. 'Presumably, they think that beating up anglers helps their cause.'

'Not sure it does,' said Gallagher. 'What happened?'

Harris glanced at Leckie.

'The first guy was heading back to his car at dusk when a couple of blokes attacked him with baseball bats,' said Leckie. 'Broke three of his ribs. The second attack happened a couple of days later on. Same scenario but it happened in broad daylight. He ended up with a fractured skull.'

'Nasty,' said Gallagher. 'You got anyone for it?'

'Not yet.'

'I'm sure you will,' said Gallagher. 'Anyway, I'll leave you to enjoy the rest of your day.'

Harris returned his phone to his pocket and opened his haversack, produced a camping stove and busied himself making tea while Leckie set up two folding chairs then stroked Scoot's head as Archie watched with undisguised jealousy. Leckie looked wistfully towards the bend in the river again.

'So, if it's that good, how come we can't fish it?' he asked.

'Because that section of the river is under new management and it's strictly private. The new owner of the Langdon Estate enforces it very aggressively.'

'What's his story then?'

'Used to work in the City. Goes by the name of Sebastian de la Roche and claims that his family is descended from French nobility, although he's no more French than you or me.' Harris took teabags out of a pouch in his haversack and dropped them into a couple of mugs. 'He bought the estate six months ago and has caused a lot of bad feeling locally ever since. The family that owned the estate before him had owned it for the best part of a century. They were old school, part of the community, happy to let local anglers fish it at a reduced cost.'

'And this La Roche character is not as community-spirited as they were?'

'He's certainly not. His first decision was to announce that no one fishes on his stretch of the river at anything but full price and that anyone entering his land without permission will be prosecuted for trespass. He's already taken action against three local fishermen.'

'I see what you mean about him making himself unpopular,' said Leckie.

'What made it worse was that he sacked the old boy who had been the estate's water bailiff for thirty years and replaced him with a nasty piece of work called Ronny Carroll. There have been several confrontations with local anglers and one of them claimed that Carroll hit him with his walking stick.'

'You get him into court?'

'It was his word against Carroll's and neither me nor Matty could persuade the CPS to take the risk. I kind of understand where they were coming from. We need to take the man down a peg or two but have to be sure that we can make it stick when we do.'

'*Tales of the Riverbank* seem to have turned somewhat darker over recent months,' said Leckie. 'How are you with La Roche? It doesn't exactly sound like a meeting of minds.'

'It certainly isn't. Not long after he bought the estate, he gave a damn-fool interview to the local newspaper in which he said that otters should be culled.' Harris, part of whose job in charge of CID was acting as the area's wildlife officer, shook his head. 'Unbelievable.'

'What was his reason?' asked Leckie.

'He had applied for planning permission to dig a couple of ponds and told the paper that the otters will target the fish unless something is done to control numbers.'

'I take it that you challenged what he said?'

'I certainly did. Rang the newspaper and demanded the right of reply.' Harris produced a packet of dog biscuits from his haversack and tossed treats to the eager animals. 'I said that he had clearly never heard of fences. The paper put it on the front page and La Roche was livid but it needed saying. The otters only came back to the river ten years ago and, even though the population has grown, their recovery is still fragile.'

Leckie nodded; the two men had bonded over their love of wildlife and enthusiasm for fishing when they met after Harris joined Greater Manchester Police and the friendship had continued when Harris moved back to work in the valley. Now, before they could continue the conversation, the kettle started to whistle. Harris was about to pick it up when he spotted a man walking along the opposite bank of the river. Harris scowled. Thin with weasel features and glinting eyes partly concealed beneath a wide-brimmed hat, the man had a carved walking stick and was accompanied by an equally mean-looking lurcher which walked with a slight limp and curled its lip as it cast evil glances in the direction of Scoot and Archie.

'Who's that?' asked Leckie. 'And what on earth is that with him?'

'That,' said Harris as he poured hot water into the mugs, 'is Ronny Carroll and the delightful Rasp. He's as notorious as his owner. A right mean bastard.'

Carroll stopped walking for a few moments and gave the inspector a wicked grin before continuing on his way along the path, followed by his limping dog, which continued to cast frequent wicked glances at Scoot and Archie over his shoulder.

'What was that about?' asked Leckie.

'I hate to think,' replied Harris. 'He's always up to something, is Ronny. None of it good.'

After finishing their drinks, the friends moved downstream and with nothing else having happened to disturb their fishing, their conversation drifted away from Ronny Carroll and his cur onto more pleasant subjects. Having thoroughly enjoyed the hours in each other's company, the friends brought their day to an end shortly before 3:00pm and after dividing up the fish, Leckie headed south to Manchester while Harris drove his white Land Rover along the main valley road in the direction of his home, a cottage high up on a hill several miles from the market town of Levton Bridge, where he worked at divisional headquarters.

The inspector had just turned the vehicle onto the rough track leading up to the cottage when his mobile phone rang. It was Gallagher.

'Matty lad,' said Harris, taking the call. 'What can I do for you this time?'

'Sorry to call again,' said the detective sergeant. 'I know you said that you weren't to be disturbed but you need to know about this. Are you still on the river?'

'No, I've just got home.'

'Then you might want to go back. A body has been found on the riverbank at the Langdon Estate. It sounds like murder.'

Harris thought of the wicked smile on Ronny Carroll's face earlier in the day.

'Who found him?' he asked.

'A young lad from the office.'

'Not Ronny Carroll then?'

'What makes you say that?' asked the sergeant.

'Because me and Leckie saw him on the riverbank this morning.'

'It wasn't him. However, I am wondering if the dead guy might be a fisherman and if there is a connection with what you and Leckie were talking about earlier?'

'It's certainly a thought,' said Harris. He started to reverse his vehicle back towards the main valley road. 'And not a very pleasant one, at that.'

Chapter two

Many questions raced through Jack Harris's mind as he stared down at the dead man sprawled on the riverside path, half a mile inside the southern boundary of the Langdon Estate. The first question was the most obvious one – who was he? Aged in his mid-thirties, and dressed in camouflage trousers and black T-shirt, he gave the impression of a military man. Harris looked at the lean face, closely shaved dark hair and wiry frame, and wondered what he had done to deserve such a violent death. And what was a man like that doing on a riverbank in the North Pennines anyway? Was it a coincidence that the murder had occurred not long after two similar assaults in Greater Manchester? And, if he was a fisherman, where was his gear?

The inspector's reverie was disturbed by a comment from one of the two other men standing looking at the body; Detective Sergeant Matthew Gallagher, a decade younger than his boss, stocky with thinning black hair which gave him, some said, the appearance of a monk.

'He doesn't look like an angler,' said the sergeant. 'He's got no gear for starters.'

'I reckon you're right,' said Harris. The inspector focused his attention on the dried blood caked around the ugly wound on the victim's forehead then glanced at the white-haired man standing to his left. Home Office pathologist Professor James Rokeby was leaning on his walking stick and perusing the body as he gathered his thoughts before conducting a more detailed examination. 'No prizes for guessing what killed him then, Doc?'

'Not really,' said the pathologist. 'I'll have to do a full post-mortem to be sure, of course, but it looks like the blow to the head, alright.'

'Any idea what was used?'

'Some kind of blunt object,' said the pathologist. He gestured towards a couple of trees further along the path that had been brought down by a gale the previous month. 'A branch from one of them might do the job.'

'How about a walking stick?' suggested Gallagher. 'Could something like that have been used?'

'Anything like that can kill you if enough force is used. Any particular reason why you want to know about a walking stick?'

'He's thinking about Ronny Carroll,' said Harris. 'He's a nasty piece of work. However, I'd rather that we did not jump to conclusions, Matty lad.'

'It's difficult not to think of him, isn't it, though?' said Gallagher. He looked upstream at a wooden sign nailed to a tree which bore the crudely-depicted words *Trespassers Will Be Prosecuted – No Exceptions* painted in red above the image of a skull. 'This *is* the area that he patrols, he *does* have a hefty walking stick and there have been several confrontations with fishermen trespassing in recent weeks, have there not?'

'There have,' conceded Harris. He looked down at the dead man. 'It would help if we knew who our victim was. Are you sure he doesn't have any ID on him?'

'Positive. No wallet. No driving licence. Clearly, whoever did this to him did not want to give us anything to go on when it came to his identity.'

'Or the John Doe himself wanted to remain a mystery for some reason,' said Harris. 'Any idea how long he's been dead, Doc?'

'I reckon it happened around about lunchtime. I should be able to be more precise after the post-mortem.'

Harris frowned; it was a troubling thought that the victim was meeting his fate in such a brutal way at the same time as the inspector and Leckie were sitting further along the same riverbank, innocently engaging in idle banter as they enjoyed their sandwiches.

'The young estate worker who found the body,' said the inspector, looking at Gallagher, 'what do we know about him?'

'He's called Danny Brewster.' The sergeant gestured towards a young woman with short blonde hair and wearing a dark suit, who was walking towards them along the riverbank. 'Ask Alison about him. She took his statement.'

'Alison,' said Harris as Detective Constable Butterfield walked up to them. 'This lad who found the body, what was he doing down here?'

'Taking pictures of the river,' said the constable. 'He looks after the estate's website and social media accounts, Facebook and Instagram mainly. Sebastian de la Roche likes the pictures to keep changing.'

'Yes, well, I don't want news of our dead guy plastered all over the Internet,' said Harris. 'Not yet anyway.'

'I don't think it'll be a problem,' said Butterfield. 'La Roche has already told Danny not to mention it online. For some reason, he thinks that having dead people lying around is not good for business.'

'What do you make of Danny?' asked the inspector.

'There's no way he was responsible for the murder, if that's what you are thinking.' Butterfield looked at the body. 'Our man looks like he could handle himself and Danny's eight stone, wet through.'

'Well, *someone* killed him,' said Harris. 'So, for the moment, we rule no one out.'

'Ronny Carroll has got to be our best bet, hasn't he?' said Butterfield.

She looked at Gallagher, who nodded in agreement.

'I reckon we should nick him now,' he said.

Before Harris could reply, two men appeared further down the riverside path. The detectives recognised one of them as Sebastian de la Roche, a tall, elegant man in a Barbour jacket, slim with strongly defined facial features and thinning dark hair streaked with grey, a man who gave the impression of someone who was keen to be viewed as a country gentleman. With him was Ronny Carroll, still with the wicked glint in his eyes, and Rasp, limping lean and mean at his heels.

'The man of the moment,' murmured Gallagher.

'Just keep it civil,' said Harris, noting the sergeant's disgusted expression. 'I know you don't like the man but please make an effort.'

'Not like him? That's the understatement of the year. I loathe him. I don't like bullies and it offends my professional pride that we've not been able to get him locked up.'

'Same here, Matty lad, but this promises to be an awkward enough investigation without antagonising either of them even further. There's already enough politics going round and the last thing I want is another complaint saying that we are victimising Ronny Carroll over the set-tos with anglers.'

Gallagher did not reply but as the two men drew closer, he contented himself with sneaking a look at the bailiff's walking stick. He was disappointed to see that it appeared to be clear of blood. Sebastian de la Roche nodded towards the body then looked at Harris.

'Have you found out who he is yet?' he asked. 'Or what he was doing here?'

'We rather hoped that you would be able to tell us,' said Harris.

'I have never seen him before,' said La Roche. He looked at his water bailiff. 'You don't know him, do you, Ronny?'

'Na.'

'Sure he's not one of the trespassers with whom you have had all the trouble recently?' asked Harris.

'I ain't had no trouble with trespassers,' said Carroll.

'Really?' said Harris.

'Yeah, really,' retorted Carroll with a scowl. 'You calling me a liar?'

'I'm just asking.'

'Yeah, well, I didn't kill him, if that's what you are thinking,' said Carroll angrily. He jabbed a finger at the inspector. 'And I'll thank you not to go round telling people that I did, neither! What's more—'

La Roche laid a restraining hand on the bailiff's arm.

'That will do,' he said. 'I am sure that the police are not accusing anyone here of being involved in this poor man's death. Isn't that right, Chief Inspector?'

'We're not blaming anyone, Sebastian, but he was killed on your land and there has been conflict between Ronny and some of the local fisherman, so you can't really be surprised that we are asking these kinds of questions, can you now?'

La Roche gave the slightest of nods to acknowledge the fact.

'Just out of idle curiosity,' said the inspector, 'where were the two of you at about lunchtime?'

'I had a run into Roxham to attend to some business,' said La Roche. 'An 11:30 appointment with the bank manager and lunch with my solicitor in the café in the marketplace. I got back about half an hour ago. I am sure that they will confirm it, if you feel the need to ask them.'

'And what about you, Ronny?' asked Harris. 'I saw you on the riverbank at just before ten. Where did you go after that?'

'To the far end of the estate to fix a fence.'

'Anyone able to confirm that you were actually there?'

'I was alone, but if you go and look at it, you'll see that it's fixed,' said Carroll. 'But like I said, I had nowt to do with what's happened.'

La Roche gestured towards the body.

'How long will he be there, anyway?' he asked.

'Not much longer,' said the pathologist. 'We'll be taking him to the mortuary at Roxham General so that I can conduct a post-mortem.'

La Roche looked at Harris.

'And your lot,' he said, 'I take it that they will be gone soon, as well?'

'I very much doubt it,' said the inspector. 'We'll be closing this stretch of the riverbank and no one will be able to fish here until our officers have finished searching it.'

'And how long will that be?' asked La Roche, pursing his lips.

'As long as it takes.'

'Yes, well, I've got a party coming down from Scotland in the morning,' said La Roche. 'It's very late notice to cancel their fishing trip so I would very much appreciate it if—'

'It's not the kind of job you can rush.'

'This is all very inconvenient,' said La Roche. 'Cancelling things is not good for the reputation of a business and could cost me a lot of money. Is there any chance that you can avoid mentioning Langdon when you tell the media what has happened? The damage to our reputation...'

'I don't care about your reputation,' said Harris. 'And the press release will have to say where the body was found, whether you like it or not.'

La Roche opened his mouth to continue his protest but the detective's stern expression persuaded him to remain silent so he satisfied himself with glowering at the inspector.

'Right,' said Harris. 'I want to have a chat with Danny Brewster. Where will I find him at this time of day?'

Butterfield looked at her boss in surprise.

'I've already talked to him,' she said. 'I took a statement.'

'I know you did, but I want to talk to him as well.' Harris looked at La Roche. 'Where am I likely to find him, Sebastian?'

'I'd rather you didn't talk to him,' said La Roche.

'Why not?' asked Harris suspiciously. 'What are you afraid he might say?'

'I'm not worried about him saying anything but he's already upset enough. He's only a young lad and he'd never seen a dead body before. As his employer, I have a duty of care towards him and I promised his mother that I'd look after him.'

'We can always do it down at the police station, if you would prefer?' said Harris.

La Roche scowled at him.

'You'll find him in the office,' he said. 'And might I say that I have been less that impressed with your attitude since you got here?'

Harris did not respond to the comment and the estate owner turned on his heel and headed back along the path, followed by Ronny Carroll and his limping dog.

'Now I understand what you mean about not antagonising them any further,' said Gallagher. 'Very diplomatic.'

The sergeant immediately regretted the comment when Harris gave him a sharp look but did not reply. Instead, he turned his attention to Butterfield.

'Right,' he said. 'I'm going to see Danny Brewster.'

'I'm not sure I see the point of talking to him again,' she said. Her voice had an offended tone. 'I asked all the right questions, you know.'

'I am sure you did but I still want to talk to him,' replied Harris. There was an edge to his voice, something that was not lost on Gallagher.

Butterfield was about to continue the argument when she noticed that the sergeant was giving her one of his warning looks. Like his boss, Gallagher did not object to young detectives offering their opinions, just so long as they went about it the right way. Butterfield, however, had developed a reputation for annoying senior officers with her forthright way of speaking and he was forever urging her to adopt a less confrontational tone.

Acutely aware that he had just ignored his own rule, he hoped that the constable would get the message that things needed to be dialled down and dialled down quickly. He knew only too well from past experience during his time serving with the Metropolitan Police, that small police teams needed to be tight-knit units and the last thing he wanted was to see tension created at the beginning of an investigation.

'Of course, I could be wrong,' said Butterfield quickly, trying to sound more respectful. 'I'm sure that talking to Danny again would be useful.'

Gallagher gave a sigh of relief and Harris, who had noticed the interchange between sergeant and constable, gave Butterfield what he hoped was a reassuring look.

'I'm sure that you did everything right,' he said. 'It's just that talking to someone else can help people remember things. I know that you both want us to lift Ronny Carroll but, given his ability to wheedle his way out of trouble on previous occasions, I am not prepared to steam in and arrest him without any evidence. It's obvious that we're not going to get anything out of La Roche and Carroll so anything else that we can get from other members of staff,

Danny Brewster included, could be invaluable. That's all I'm saying.'

Pinch point avoided, Gallagher nodded in agreement and Butterfield relaxed when she realised that she was not in trouble.

'Just wait until you meet the office manager then,' she said. 'She's a right dragon!'

The constable's comment lifted the mood and Harris and Gallagher were still smiling as they followed La Roche and Carroll along the winding path that led to the centre of the estate.

Chapter three

In normal circumstances, Jack Harris would have relished the walk through the sun-dappled woodland with its abundant birdsong and splashes of colour from clusters of wildflowers, but this time his mind was occupied with darker thoughts, mainly a nagging feeling that, despite the argument in favour of Ronny Carroll as the murderer, the investigation would prove to be more complicated than it might at first appear.

After fifteen minutes' walking, the officers emerged from the wood and entered a walled yard, at one end of which stood an ivy-covered Victorian house and a collection of stone outbuildings, which included the estate office, outside which had gathered the police search team. They were being addressed by a dark-haired, middle-aged woman with a matronly appearance and Harris gave a satisfied smile; Detective Inspector Gillian Roberts always provided a reassuring presence. The organiser on Harris's team, she was the one that he relied on to take care of the logistics. She concluded her briefing and walked over to Harris.

'I reckon we'll have two or three hours of searching before we start to lose the light,' she said. 'Anything you need us to do first?'

'Can you double-check that we've got statements from all the staff and that they're all corroborated, particularly Ronny Carroll's claim that he was mending a fence at the other end of the estate when our John Doe was being murdered? He says there was no one with him.'

'Shouldn't we have lifted him already?' said Roberts. 'It's not like you to be indecisive.'

'It's too easy. Too obvious.'

'Sometimes it *is* obvious,' said Roberts. 'Ronny had motive and opportunity and no one to support his alibi.'

'You may be right. Let's double-check his story before we bring him in, though. You can leave the office manager to me and I'll talk to the young lad who found the body as well.'

'Danny Brewster, isn't it?'

'You know him?'

'He was a year ahead of my eldest at Roxham Comp. A decent enough kid, from what my son said about him. He's a bit of an IT whizz. Ended up as good as running the school website and spends most of his spare time playing computer games. That's how my son knows him. They were in the same after-school club. But hasn't Alison already taken his statement?'

'Don't you start,' said Harris.

He headed off to join Butterfield, who was waiting at the entrance to the estate office. On entering the room, the detectives were met by a middle-aged woman in dark-framed spectacles that gave her a severe, disapproving appearance. Something told Harris that it was not an act; Miranda Jacobs looked genuinely irritated at the intrusion.

'Can I help you?' she asked in clipped tones that suggested that she hoped the answer was 'no'.

'I'm DCI Harris,' said the inspector.

He held up his warrant card so that she could identify him but the office manager did not bother to look at it.

'I know who you are,' she replied. 'What do you want?'

'To talk to Danny.'

'Your colleague has already talked to him,' said Jacobs. She nodded at Butterfield.

'Yes, well, I want to talk to him as well,' said Harris.

'If you think it's necessary,' said the manager.

'I do, yes.'

Jacobs gestured towards a door.

'He's in the rest room,' she said. 'But be careful with him. He's very upset by what has happened.'

The detectives walked into the rest room to find Brewster sitting on a sofa. The teenager was pale and looked nervously at the officers, their stern expressions doing little to ease anxiety which was further exacerbated by the fact that the inspector was a big man whose size could often be intimidating. Sitting next to Brewster, and eying him with concern, was a woman in her mid-twenties with short dark hair, wearing thick-rimmed spectacles. Harris showed his warrant card.

'DCI Harris,' he said. He looked at the woman. 'And you are?'

'Janice Garvey,' she said. 'I'm an administrative assistant here. I thought that someone should sit with Danny. He's very upset, as you can see. What do you want with him?'

'To ask a couple of questions,' said Harris.

'I told her everything I know,' protested the teenager, gesturing to Butterfield. 'There's nothing else.'

'People remember things,' said Harris. He pulled a chair close to the teenager and sat down. Sweat was glistening on Brewster's brow. 'You seem nervous, Danny. Something worrying you?'

'What do you think? I've never seen a dead body before. Or been interviewed by the police.'

'It's nothing to worry about,' said Harris. 'Just take me through what happened.'

The teenager gave himself a few moments to regain his composure.

'I went down to the river to take some pictures,' he said eventually. 'Mr de la Roche likes me to change them on the website as much as I can because it makes it easier for the search engines to find it and the shadows were really atmospheric this afternoon. I had just got there when I saw the body. It was awful.'

Brewster shuddered at the memory and his voice was so quiet that the detectives had to lean forward and listen closely to make out what he was saying.

'He was just lying there with his head all stoved in,' he said.

'And you didn't see anyone else?' asked the inspector.

'No.'

'And you don't know who he is?'

Brewster shook his head.

'When did this happen?' asked Harris.

'Just after two o'clock.'

'And earlier in the day?' asked Harris. 'Where were you then? Say, about lunchtime?'

'*She* asked me that as well,' said Brewster, looking at Butterfield. 'Why do you want to know that? Am I a suspect?'

'No. I ask because we think that's when the murder happened and we are asking everyone where they were.'

Brewster relaxed slightly.

'I was in the office,' he said. 'Having my sandwiches.'

'Can anyone confirm that?' asked Harris.

'I can,' said Janice Garvey. 'We usually have lunch together.'

'It's in her statement,' said Butterfield.

'And neither of you went out onto the riverbank at that time?' asked the inspector.

Brewster and Garvey shook their heads.

'OK, fair enough,' said Harris.

He stood up and headed for the door. Once he and Butterfield were back in the yard, the constable glanced at her boss.

'Why are you so interested in Danny?' she asked. 'You don't really think that Danny killed him, do you?'

'Like I keep saying, for the moment we rule no one out.'

***

An hour later, the inspector was heading back down the valley road in the Land Rover when his mobile rang.

'It's Leckie,' said the voice on the other end. 'I heard something on the radio about your dead guy. If you want, I'll pull together everything I know about our riverbank incidents and email it over. You never know, it might turn out to be useful...'

Chapter four

Just before dawn the next day, Jack Harris fed the dogs and had a couple of slices of toast and a mug of tea. Then they walked a couple of miles across the hills surrounding their home. As the strengthening light revealing more of the landscape, the inspector appreciated, as he always did, the fact that he could not see any sign of human habitation from his cottage. Situated halfway up a hill, the house was out of sight of the main valley road. The inspector had stumbled across it not long after returning to work in the area. The property's sense of solitude appealed to something deep within him and he had spent six months renovating the cottage before moving in.

Having returned from the walk, Harris loaded the dogs into the back of his white Land Rover and negotiated the rough track that wound its way down to the main valley road. After driving the short distance to Levton Bridge, he parked halfway up the road leading to the marketplace, outside the Victorian building that housed the divisional police headquarters. As he walked up the steps to the front entrance, followed by the dogs, he waved aside the questions from the small group of journalists that had already gathered, having been attracted by the force's press release about the murder. Harris knew that many more would join them as news spread about the murder and he scowled at the thought; the inspector had never felt at ease when dealing with the media and he was relieved when he entered the station and could no longer hear the reporters' shouted protests at his refusal to engage with them.

After punching in the security code for the door leading from reception, he headed for his first-floor office where he filled up the dogs' water bowl and started checking his emails. His desk phone rang and he picked up the receiver.

'It's Doc,' said a voice.

'You're in early. You got an ID on our John Doe yet?'

'Not yet. His fingerprints are not on record so I'm going to send a DNA sample away but the lab is up to its ears so we'll not get the results for several days, assuming that he's on record somewhere. I was actually ringing to ask if you wanted to attend the post-mortem. Can you get down here for half ten?'

'Yeah, fine, see you then.'

Harris had only just replaced the receiver when the phone rang again and he sighed as he glanced at the dogs.

'It's going to be one of those days,' he said, and picked up the receiver. It was Leckie.

'I've sent that stuff on the Anti-Fishing Alliance,' he said. 'Your La Roche guy is just the kind of target they like so it's not beyond the bounds of possibility that they have a go at him one day.'

'It certainly isn't,' said Harris.

He spent the next ten minutes reading the file then looked up just in time to see Gallagher walking past his door. 'Matty lad! Come and take a look at this.'

The sergeant walked into his office and looked over his boss's shoulder as Harris opened a picture attachment.

'This from Leckie?' asked Gallagher.

'Yeah,' said the inspector as the picture emerged of an earnest-looking woman in her mid-twenties, with short-cropped black hair, wearing thick-rimmed spectacles and dungarees. She was standing on a riverbank that neither detective recognised. 'That's Miriam Coles. She's the one who set up the AFA to campaign for fishing to be banned. Don't be fooled by the respectable appearance, she's as hardline as they come.'

The inspector opened a second attachment; a grainy image of an unshaven man with dirty, unkempt curly hair, wearing a tattered jumper. He was standing in a field and reminded Gallagher of Russell Brand.

'And this delightful individual is?' asked the sergeant.

'Guy Robertson, a university dropout who lives in a squat in Manchester with Miriam. They founded the Anti-Fishing Alliance together but Miriam is their public face for obvious reasons,' said Harris. He opened a Word attachment. 'I'll print out the file for you.'

Gallagher made them mugs of tea then settled down to read the document as Harris continued to check his emails. Leckie's report stated that Miriam Coles had been born in Buckinghamshire, was twenty-six years old and had been well brought-up as part of a good family, her father a stockbroker, her mother a headteacher. She had attended Roedean School where she showed herself to be a keen follower of equestrian sports; there was even talk that she might be good enough to represent Great Britain at the Olympics. On leaving school, her father had arranged for her to take up a job at a public relations company run by an old school friend of his in Manchester but she fell in with Guy Robertson after meeting him at a party, quit the job and moved into the squat. They created the Anti-Fishing Alliance a few months later and in addition to several assaults on anglers, it was also suspected of setting fire to a couple of clubhouses belonging to angling clubs as well as slashing tyres. Gallagher looked up from the document and shook his head.

'How come a nice girl like that ended up doing all this?' he asked. 'I mean, she was a nice middle-class girl who had everything going for her, wasn't she?'

'She was but she wouldn't be the first to reject her privileged upbringing. Think Patty Hearst and all that. She'll be carrying a machine gun and robbing banks soon.'

'And how come she's so interested in fishing? This suggests that horses are more her thing.'

'If you look on the next page, you'll see that she gave an interview to a student newspaper in which she recounted a story from when she was a small child and saw a trout being hooked by a fisherman. She claims that she saw the agony in its eyes and still has nightmares about it. It's all cobblers, of course. There's plenty of research that says that fish do not experience pain when they are caught.'

'I suspect there's a lot of people would disagree.'

'Don't you start,' said Harris. However, the comment was not a rebuke and was accompanied with a slight smile.

Gallagher placed the report on the desk. 'And you reckon there might be a link between this bunch and our murder, do you?' he asked.

'According to Leckie, they are on the lookout for new targets and Sebastian de la Roche's fishing estate is the kind of thing they go for. It's worth bearing in mind.'

There was a knock on the door and Gillian Roberts walked into the office. Harris looked hopefully at the detective inspector.

'Any news?' he asked.

'I got a couple of the lads to check the fence that Ronny said he had fixed,' she said. 'It has certainly been repaired and the wood looks fresh. Having said that, I reckon the job would have only taken a couple of hours and he hasn't said anything to account for the rest of his day and neither has anyone else.'

Harris looked at Gallagher but the sergeant resumed his reading of Leckie's intelligence report; he had no desire to reignite the previous day's tension.

'Anything else I should know?' Harris asked Roberts.

'Not a lot. The Ministry of Defence are checking but the guy I talked to did not sound very hopeful. He said we weren't giving him much to go on.' Roberts gestured at the document resting on Gallagher's lap. 'Anything interesting?'

'It's some stuff that Leckie sent about the AFA,' said Harris.

'Ah, the fragrant *Ms* Coles,' said Roberts.

'You know her?' asked Gallagher.

'I've not met her but I know her mum. I went to Roxham Comp with Margie. She lives in Leeds now but I still get the odd phone call from her. She's in despair about Miriam. Why so interested?'

Before Harris could reply, the inspector's desk phone rang and he picked up the receiver, listened for a few moments, said 'I'll be there in half an hour' and put the receiver back down.

'That was Ross Makin,' he said. 'He thinks he knows the identity of our dead man.'

'And how would the director of the Three Valleys Wildlife Trust know that?' asked Roberts.

'He doesn't want to discuss it on the phone,' said Harris. He stood up and unhooked his jacket from the back of his chair. 'He sounded worried. Matty, you OK to go with me to attend the post-mortem in Roxham? We can pop in on Ross on the way.'

'Sure,' said Gallagher. 'You'll have to run the gauntlet of reporters, though, and they didn't look happy. They were giving you pelters. They reckon you're not giving them enough information.'

Roberts gave Harris a sly look.

'Glad to see that the money was well spent on that media course the commander insisted you take,' she said. 'Well worth it.'

'Yes, thank you,' said Harris, giving her a pained look. However, he had taken the comment in the spirit in which it was intended and the look was followed by a smile in Gallagher's direction. 'No bloody respect for seniority, Matty lad, that's the problem with the modern police force. Come on, let's go and see what Ross has for us.'

The inspector stood up, gave a couple of clicks of the tongue to instruct the dogs to follow him, and left the room.

Chapter five

An hour later, Harris guided the Land Rover down off the moors and approached the county town of Roxham, the largest settlement in the area. Just before he and Gallagher entered the town's outskirts, the inspector turned onto a road that led to a woodland nature reserve. He parked outside the Wildlife Trust's headquarters, a single-storey timber-framed building with solar panels on its roof and birds thronging round the feeders hanging from a series of poles.

The detectives reported to reception and, having left Scoot and Archie to be fussed over by the staff, they headed for Ross Makin's office, where they were welcomed by a tall, dark-haired man in his thirties. The director gestured for them to take a seat and eyed them uneasily across his desk for a few moments.

'You look worried,' said Harris.

'I am,' said Makin. 'Events would seem to have taken a somewhat sinister turn. Your dead man, is he in his mid-thirties, slim with short dark hair?'

Harris reached into his jacket pocket, produced his smartphone and called up the photograph he had taken before the body was moved the previous evening. He held the device up so that Makin could see.

'Is that him?' he asked.

'I haven't met him but it's like the description I was given,' said Makin. 'I reckon it's Carl Bradby.'

'Who is he and what was he doing on the Langdon Estate?' asked Harris.

'I am afraid that I have been holding out on you, Jack,' said Makin unhappily. 'And I have this awful feeling that if I had told you what I knew right from the start, this poor man might not have died.'

'Told me what?' asked Harris.

'Follow me,' said Makin. He stood up and headed for the door. 'There's something you need to see.'

He led the intrigued detectives out of the office and along a corridor to a room at the back of the building, in the corner of which stood a chest freezer. Harris glanced at Gallagher, who shrugged in bemusement. Makin opened the freezer and removed an object in a large cellophane bag, which he placed on a nearby table. The detectives could see that it was the body of a dead otter, around whose neck was the livid wound left by the snare that had throttled the life out of the animal as it struggled desperately to break free. Every movement had remorselessly tightened the wire noose until the creature breathed its tormented final breath. Harris scowled; having more affinity with animals than humans, he felt a sharp tug of emotion as he looked at the dead creature.

'A terrible way to die,' he said.

Makin nodded.

'Where was it found?' asked Gallagher. Born and bred in London, and having worked for the Metropolitan Police before he and his wife moved north to be close to her elderly parents, he had little interest in wildlife but his expression showed that he was equally appalled by what he was witnessing. 'And what has it got to do with this Bradby fellow?'

'Carl found it dumped on the Langdon Estate,' said Makin.

'How come?' asked Harris.

'Because he knew it was there. He had been hired by an animal rights group to expose Sebastian de la Roche for the man he really is.'

'That'll be the Anti-Fishing Alliance, I take it?' said Gallagher.

'Actually, it was Dark Waters,' said Makin.

'Dark Waters?' said Gallagher. He looked at Harris. 'Weren't they mentioned in Leckie's report?'

The inspector nodded.

'I take it that was something about *Ms* Coles?' said Makin.

'Do you know her?' asked Gallagher.

'Just by reputation. She and her pals were supporters of Dark Waters but decided that it wasn't radical enough and left to set up the AFA.'

'So, what actually is Dark Waters?' asked Gallagher.

'They were founded by a man called Stuart Liversedge and his wife Anna,' said Harris. 'They campaign against anything that harms rivers, pollution, riverbed dredging, persecution of wildlife, that sort of thing.'

'And anglers,' said Makin, shooting the inspector a sly look. 'Boy, do they hate anglers with a passion. Eh, Jack?'

Harris ignored the comment.

'I don't get all this anti-fishing stuff,' said Gallagher. He looked at his boss. 'Aren't you always saying that most anglers are conservationists?'

'And so they are,' said Harris. 'But Stuart and his wife run a sanctuary for injured waterfowl in Scotland and they became increasingly angry at the number of birds being brought in having been harmed by discarded nets and hooks. Stuart has been very outspoken on the subject. He reckons that if anglers cannot be trusted to clean up after themselves, the sport should be banned.'

'A point on which he and the AFA clearly agree,' said Gallagher.

'It's just about the only thing,' said Makin. 'There's no love lost between the two groups. Stuart believes that the use of violence makes for bad PR and alienates the public.'

'He's probably right,' said Gallagher. 'How come Dark Waters are hiring investigators like this Bradby fellow?'

'Because they act like they are a law unto themselves,' said Harris with a scowl. 'Which is why I do not get on particularly well with them. If they hear about someone doing something illegal, they won't bring it to us, they'll investigate it themselves and publish the results on social media. They've gone for all sorts, landowners, farmers, fishing clubs, the lot, all funded by donations from the public, which is why they are so sensitive about violence.'

'How come they won't work with the police?' asked Gallagher.

'Stuart's view is that, if the police did their job properly, Dark Waters wouldn't need to get involved,' said Harris.

'He's right, isn't he?' said Gallagher.

'And what exactly does that mean?' said Harris, giving the sergeant a sharp look.

Gallagher cursed inwardly at having made the unguarded comment at a time when he had resolved to avoid such actions. He knew that it was a sensitive subject for his boss, so chose his next words carefully.

'Aren't you always saying that the top brass don't give wildlife crime the priority that it deserves?' he said. 'How many times have you come out of meetings spitting bullets because Curtis would much rather you concentrate on catching the villains who are nicking farm machinery than investigating wildlife crime? Can you see him giving you clearance to spend time on a dead otter?'

'I guess not,' said Harris. He looked at Makin. 'How come you know so much about Bradby's investigation into the Langdon Estate, Ross?'

'He rang me up and asked to meet but said that he wouldn't come here and if we could meet at the car park next to Low Peak's Wood instead. It was all very cloak and dagger. He said that Dark Waters had received a tip-off that the Langdon Estate was setting snares to catch otters. He said that he'd been making a film showing how the snares were being deliberately set close to their new fish ponds.'

'And that's illegal, I take it?' said Gallagher.

'It is if they are set for otters because they are a protected species,' said Harris. 'Not, I suspect, that Sebastian de la Roche would care about that – and Ronny Carroll certainly wouldn't.'

'I did try to warn Carl that Ronny was not the type of man you wanted to cross,' said Makin. 'But he said that he'd learned how to look after himself when he was in the SAS and that he'd have no trouble handling him. Clearly, he underestimated him.'

'Let's not jump to conclusions,' said Harris. 'I suspect that Dark Waters are not short of people who don't like the way they do things. So, Bradby asked you to look after the otter for him?'

'Yeah, he did. It's all happened over a couple of weeks. He asked me to keep it in the freezer because it was evidence.' Makin placed the body back in the freezer, closed the lid and led the detectives back into the corridor. 'He said that they'd already got enough evidence but that he was going to give it another couple of days just to be sure.'

Once they had returned to the director's office, Harris gave Makin a stern look.

'I really wish that you had come to me earlier, Ross,' he said. 'I don't like people taking the law into their own hands on my patch, at the best of times, and it could have saved everyone a lot of trouble if we'd known what was happening.'

'I did think about ringing you.' A defensive tone had crept into Makin's voice. 'Honestly I did, but Carl said that Dark Waters were more likely to get a result than the police.'

'The irony is that Curtis will give you as much time as you want now,' said Gallagher. 'I mean, it could turn out to be a motive for murder, couldn't it?'

The comment cheered up Harris.

'Every cloud, eh?' he said. He looked up at the wall clock. 'We've got to go to the post-mortem. Are you OK to hold on to the otter for a little longer, Ross?'

'What do I say if Dark Waters come claiming that it's theirs?' asked Makin.

'Tell them that we have seized it as evidence in a murder investigation and that they are to leave it to the professionals.' Harris gave a devilish smile. 'This is my game now and they will have to play by my rules. Come on, Matty lad, let's go and see a body of the human variety!'

* * *

Twenty minutes later, the detectives were standing in the mortuary at Roxham General Hospital, watching the pathologist as he crouched over the body to conduct his examination.

'Your man's military career would appear to have been eventful,' said Doc eventually.

'What makes you say that?' asked Harris.

'He's got a several scars, at least two of which would appear to have been caused by a knife.' Doc pointed to the scar on Bradby's stomach. 'He was lucky that one did not kill him. A couple of centimetres to the left and it may well have done. Oh, and one of his arms was broken and did not heal properly. He would have struggled to straighten it out fully. I imagine that it was quite painful.'

'Are any of them recent injuries?' asked Gallagher.

'No, they're all pretty old,' said the pathologist. He moved on to examine the gash on the dead man's forehead. 'This is definitely what killed him. Like I said yesterday, the blow was wielded with considerable force.'

'Did he die instantly?' asked Harris.

'Pretty much. There are no defensive wounds. He probably did not know what had hit him.' The pathologist leaned closer to the body. 'Now that's interesting.'

He walked over to a side table, picked up a pair of tweezers and returned to resume his examination of the head wound. After a few moments, he held up the tweezers so that the detectives could see the small shard of wood that he had extracted.

'That's from your murder weapon,' he said. 'I'll get it analysed but it confirms that he was struck with something wooden, like a tree branch or, as you suggested, Matthew, maybe a heavy walking stick.'

'Or a fence post,' said Gallagher.

Harris was about to reply when his mobile phone rang. It was Roberts.

'Gillian,' he said. 'What news?'

'We've just had a call from a chap called Stuart Liversedge,' said the detective inspector. 'He says that he needs to talk to you and that it's urgent.'

'I'll bet it is,' said the inspector.

Chapter six

Harris phoned the co-founder of Dark Waters as he guided the Land Rover up onto the moor road in the direction of Levton Bridge. The inspector did not expect the conversation with Stuart Liversedge to go well. Although the two men had never actually spoken to each other, they had conversed several times in recent months through letters in the Angling Times, each man putting their side of the argument for and against a ban on fishing. They had not been friendly exchanges and, eventually, the magazine's editor had requested that they tone down the language being used. Superintendent Philip Curtis, the detective's divisional commander, had similar misgivings and went one step further, ordering Harris to bring the correspondence to an end. The inspector, who would normally have resented such an intervention, found himself agreeing, recognising that the commander was right when he suggested that the correspondence ran the risk of damaging not just the inspector's reputation but that of the force, particularly if the mainstream media heard about it and it became a bigger story.

So as he made the call, Harris resolved to maintain a strictly professional approach to the conversation, which he put on speaker so that Gallagher could hear.

'Stuart Liversedge?' he asked as the call was answered.

'Jack Harris, I assume,' said a voice with the barest hint of a Scottish accent. 'We talk at last. Much better than exchanging insults on the pages of the *Angling Times*, don't you think?'

'You're probably right,' said Harris. He was relieved that he could not detect any animosity in Stuart Liversedge's voice. 'I understand that you want to talk to me?'

'I believe I know the identity of the man whose body was found on the riverbank at the Langdon Estate.'

'Are you going to tell me that it's Carl Bradby?'

'Ah, so you know,' said Stuart. 'Ross Makin tell you that, did he?'

'He did, yes, but we need you to confirm that it's definitely him.'

'I'm pretty sure that it will be,' said Liversedge. 'Ross probably told you that he was working on an investigation into the Langdon Estate for us. I was due to hear from him first thing this morning but he didn't ring and his phone is switched off. Then I heard the radio report about the body being found.'

'We're still trying to confirm that it is definitely him,' said Harris. 'Do you know who his next of kin is? A wife maybe?'

'Carl was a very secretive guy and never gave much away about his private life. He certainly did not mention a wife.'

'Parents then?'

'He never mentioned them either,' said Stuart.

'An address?' asked Harris. 'That would be a start.'

'Sorry. We used to get in touch via mobile phone. I'll text you the number but, like I say, it's been switched off.'

'Do you have bank account details then?' asked Harris. 'We can get his address that way.'

'Sorry, Carl always insisted on being paid in cash. In person.'

'You must have something if he was working for you?' said Harris. He was unable to keep the exasperation out of his voice.

'I did once ask him why he was so secretive and he said that he had to be careful in his line of work. I suppose paranoia comes with the territory for those SAS guys.'

'It does,' said Harris. As the Land Rover approached a sharp bend, the inspector saw a group of sheep clustered next to a small stone bridge, applied the brakes and edged his way past them. 'How come you employed him anyway?'

'He rang me out of the blue last year. Said that he'd set up as a freelance investigator, and asked if we would like to give him a try. We're always on the lookout for people with his kind of skills and he was excellent at what he did. It did not take him long to confirm that the Langdon Estate has been setting snares for otters.'

'How come you knew that they were doing it in the first place?' asked Harris. 'I had not heard anything about it and I'm the local wildlife liaison officer.'

'Someone messaged us through Facebook. I don't know who it was because when we checked it out, it turned out to be a fake identity. Whoever it was, they knew what they were talking about because Carl found the otter. He said he would go back to see if they did it again. I imagine that your main suspect is the water bailiff? Ronny Carroll's a nasty piece of work, from what Carl said, but can I suggest another couple of names?'

'Go on.'

'Can you come and see me and we can talk about it face to face?'

'It's a long drive,' said Harris. 'Can't we do it on the phone?'

'I'd rather not.'

'Look, I don't really have time to play games,' said Harris. Irritation had crept into his voice. 'If you've got something to tell me, I need to know it and I need to know it now.'

'I'd feel happier talking face to face.'

Harris glanced at Gallagher, who shrugged.

'OK,' said Harris with a sigh. 'If you insist, but it'll be late afternoon. I have a lot of things to sort out first.'

'I'll be here,' said Stuart.

The call at an end, the inspector glanced across at Gallagher.

'What do you make of that then, Matty lad?' he asked.

'Dark Waters run deep,' said the sergeant.

'Very poetic.'

'It must be the company I keep,' said the sergeant.

'Yeah, that'll be it,' said Harris.

Chapter seven

With much to occupy their thoughts, the detectives made the rest of the journey to Levton Bridge in near silence; the norm for Harris, a rarity for the usually talkative sergeant. Once they had returned to the police station, the inspector issued notice of a meeting for his team in the briefing room then, followed by his dogs as ever, he headed for his office to do a quick check of his emails. He had only just sat down at his desk when a slim, balding uniformed officer entered the room.

As ever, the district commander frowned when he saw the dogs curled up in their usual position beneath the radiator. However, he said nothing; Philip Curtis had learned his lesson the hard way in the early days of his tenure. Eager to stamp his authority on his first command, and acutely aware of Jack Harris's reputation for doing things his way, the superintendent issued an edict banning Scoot from the police station – the inspector only had the one dog in those days. It was an order that the chastened commander was forced to rescind two days later following protests from staff.

'Gillian tells me that we have an ID on our dead man,' said Curtis. He sat down at the desk. 'A former soldier called Carl Bradby who was investigating the Langdon Estate for its persecution of otters, I believe. That'll please you.'

'Sir?'

'Well, for once, I can't bang on about you spending too much time investigating wildlife crime, can I?' said the commander, giving a wry smile.

'I guess not,' said Harris. He returned the smile, appreciating the commander's comment. The relationship between the two men had improved dramatically since those awkward early days but both remained conscious of the need to constantly work at keeping it that way. 'Hopefully, we can wrap things up in decent time.'

'Hopefully,' said Curtis. 'Are you going to arrest Ronny Carroll? The media are bombarding the Press Office for updates and it would be nice to give them something to calm things down.'

'It might not be that simple. We have nothing definite on him and the guy who hired Carl Bradby to work for Dark Waters is hinting that there may other suspects. Matty and I are going to see him his afternoon.'

'He was the man with whom you had the correspondence in the *Angling Times*, wasn't he?'

'That's him.'

'Well, just remember that a murder inquiry is no place for personal disagreements,' said Curtis. 'In the meantime, you will have seen how many journalists are gathered outside the station. We have to give them something. Can we hold a press conference, please?'

Harris nodded without much enthusiasm but did not argue the point.

'An hour OK?' he asked.

'Fine. I'll let them know.'

Harris sighed, switched off his computer and followed the commander into the corridor; the emails would have to wait, it was time to catch up with his team. Once in the briefing room, the inspector stood at the front and scanned the faces of the plainclothes and uniformed officers.

'Where's the DI?' he asked.

'I'm here,' said Gillian Roberts, entering the room. She gestured at a slim young man in a suit, who was sitting on the front row. 'Any room for a little 'un, Alistair?'

'Sure,' said Detective Constable Alistair Marshall.

He moved his chair along to accommodate her and Roberts sat down and held up a computer printout.

'The Army have just emailed Carl Bradby's service record and it makes for very interesting reading,' she said. 'It would appear that we have a dead war hero on our hands.'

'Why do you say that?' asked Harris. He was unable to hide the scepticism from his voice. As a former military man, the inspector had always regarded the word 'hero' as overused. 'It's the job,' he would say, 'just the job.' Roberts, who had lost count of the times she had heard him say it, gave the slightest of smiles.

'Well,' she said. 'He was mentioned twice in despatches following events that took place in Afghanistan. I'm no expert on these things, but it sounds pretty heroic to me.'

'It's certainly true that they don't give them away,' said Harris. He gave a grudging nod of approval. 'Afghanistan, you say? When?'

'In 2014. The final months before UK forces withdrew, apparently.'

'A particularly chaotic time,' said Harris. 'There were plenty of men and women who displayed exceptional courage then. What did Bradby do?'

'The first incident happened six months after he transferred to the SAS,' said Roberts, referring to the printout. 'He was in a vehicle that ran over an IED, killing the driver and badly wounding one of his comrades. The Taliban surrounded the car but Bradby held them off and carried his pal to safety. The guy lost a leg but survived.'

'And the second time?'

'Seventeen days later.' Roberts ran her finger down the printout again. 'Same kind of story. He was part of a night-time surveillance operation which was surprised by the Taliban. Two of his comrades were shot dead and another was badly wounded. Bradby drove the Taliban back under heavy fire, killing three of them and allowing his comrades to carry the wounded man to safety. Sounds like there's quite a few people who owe their lives to our Mr Bradby.'

'A hero indeed,' said Gallagher.

'When did he leave the Army?' asked Harris.

'Three years ago,' replied Roberts. 'According to the officer I was talking to, he set up his private security consultancy a few months later, carrying out mainly surveillance work. My Army chap lost track of him after that but it explains why he ended up doing work for Dark Waters.'

'They're an environmental campaign group, aren't they?' said a young female plainclothes officer with a fresh complexion and close-cropped dark hair, who was sitting on the second row. Detective Constable Sally Orr was the most recent, and youngest, recruit to CID at Levton Bridge and was always eager to impress more senior officers. 'They post stuff on social media showing offences being committed.'

'They do indeed,' said Harris. 'And they are of interest to us because Carl Bradby had been hired to investigate the Langdon Estate for illegally setting snares to catch otters. You need to keep an ear out for the Anti-Fishing Alliance as well, the AFA. They're another campaign group but one with a reputation for violence.'

'Are they involved with the murder?' asked Orr.

'There's nothing to suggest that they are but the relationship with Dark Waters is a fractious one so if you hear anyone talking about either of them, I want to know about it PDQ.'

'What's the next move then?' asked Roberts.

'Matty and I are going to see Dark Waters and, while we're away, I want everyone to keep digging for anything we can find about Bradby's private life. Social security numbers, where he lived, who his friends were, the usual drill. We still know very little about him.'

Alison Butterfield pulled a face.

'Is something wrong, Constable?' asked Harris.

'It's nothing,' said Butterfield quickly, remembering the difficult conversation with the inspector on the riverbank the previous day. 'Nothing at all.'

'It didn't look like nothing,' said Harris. His tone of voice suggested he was not irritated by her comment. 'Go on, why the sour look?'

Butterfield glanced at Gallagher, who nodded.

'Well,' said Butterfield, 'I can't help thinking that we should have arrested Ronny Carroll by now. Isn't he the most likely suspect?' She looked round, seeking support from her colleagues but, even if any of them agreed, no one reacted; none of them felt like pushing their luck. 'It's obvious, isn't it?'

'It may be obvious to you,' said Harris. 'But Dark Waters say there are other suspects worth considering and I'd like to find out more before we go crashing in and arrest Carroll.'

Seeing the young constable's disappointed look, the inspector gave her a reassuring smile.

'I know that carrying out background checks is boring work,' he said. 'I used to hate it with a passion when I was a young cop. However, it's also important work, and it needs doing. Get the basics right and everything else falls into place, which is why I also want us to go back to the Langdon Estate and question every member of staff again.'

'La Roche won't be pleased to hear that,' said Roberts. 'Any particular reason?'

'Yes. They're giving each other alibis and I want to make sure that there are no gaps. Don't mention what we know about the Dark Waters investigation for the moment, let's see if anyone brings it up.' Harris noticed that Butterfield looked like she wanted to speak again but was not sure if she should risk it. 'Alison, you have something to say?'

'I don't want to sound like I'm obsessed with Ronny Carroll,' she said, 'but no one has given him an alibi. All we have is his story that he was fixing a fence but I don't think that will have taken all day.'

Harris gave a slight smile.

'Perhaps you'd like to start with him,' he said.

Butterfield beamed at the prospect.

Chapter eight

Following the briefing, Matty Gallagher grabbed an early lunch in the canteen then returned to the CID squad room, where several detectives were seated at the desks, making telephone calls and checking the Internet as they continued in their efforts to build up a more complete picture of Carl Bradby's life. After he had spent thirty minutes engaged in fruitless phone conversations, the sergeant slammed down the receiver in frustration.

'Bloody hell!' he exclaimed. 'This is getting us nowhere!'

Alison Butterfield looked over from her desk and gave him a cheeky smile.

'Now, now, Sarge,' she said. 'Background checks may be boring work but it's also important work, and it needs doing. Get the basics right and everything else falls into place.'

Gallagher gave her one of his looks.

'You really don't do yourself any favours,' he said.

She grinned.

'I take it you're not getting anywhere?' said Gallagher.

'It's like he was a non-person,' she said. 'His business does not even have a website, that I can find. I mean, who has a business but no website?'

'Did you get anywhere with his mobile phone?' asked Gallagher.

'Afraid not,' said Butterfield. 'When we finally tracked down the right service provider, they double-checked the address in Peterborough that he gave their accounts department but it turns out to be an old one and he had not been there for a while.'

'Did the phone company not get suspicious?'

'He kept paying the bills so they had no reason to worry.'

'What about Companies House?' asked the sergeant. 'Did you check them, like I suggested?'

'I did, yeah. He gave another address in Peterborough but it was made-up – the local cops checked it out for us but it's a patch of wasteland that's been derelict for years. Bradby did give them a genuine landline phone number for his business but I rang it and it's on answerphone only.'

Gallagher walked across to look over her shoulder, he produced his notebook from his pocket and jotted down the number.

'We need to find that answerphone,' he said, returning to his desk.

Butterfield glanced round to make sure that Harris had not entered the room without her noticing.

'I know it came out wrong back there in the briefing, and that there may be other suspects, but shouldn't we be arresting Ronny Carroll anyway? The longer we hold off, the more chance there is that he will do a runner, isn't there?' She looked round the room, again seeking support from her colleagues. 'I'm right, aren't I?'

This time, in the absence of Jack Harris, there were nodding heads.

'*Now* you support me,' said Butterfield.

All eyes turned to Gallagher.

'You heard the DCI,' said the sergeant. 'He wants us to hold off until he gives the word and that's what we'll do.'

He gave Butterfield a hard look.

'Understood?' he said.

'Understood,' said Butterfield with a heavy sigh. 'I guess I just want to get out of these boring checks and do something useful.'

'Amen to that,' said Alistair Marshall.

The sergeant's desk phone rang and he picked up the receiver. 'DS Gallagher.'

'This is Jane Randall,' said the caller. 'I work for the council in Hemel Hempstead. You asked us to check the electoral roll for the address that Mr Bradby gave the Army for his parents when he enlisted.'

'I did,' said Gallagher. He reached for his pad and pen. 'Any luck?'

'I am afraid not,' she said. 'We can't find any evidence that they have lived there after 2009. I'm sorry that we cannot be more helpful.'

'Thanks for trying, anyway,' said Gallagher. He ended the call, replaced the receiver, tossed his pen across the table in frustration then looked at Butterfield. 'But I take your point.'

He looked at the wall clock, stood up and unhooked his jacket from the back of his chair.

'I'd better be making tracks,' he said. 'It's a three-hour drive to Stuart Liversedge's place, apparently.'

'Better than being stuck in here,' said Marshall.

'Except that Harris will have done his press conference by then and he'll be in a foul mood, like he always is after doing stuff with journalists,' said Gallagher.

When he arrived at the front of the police station, Harris was still holding his press conference on the steps. As Gallagher leaned against the inspector's Land Rover and watched proceedings, it quickly became clear that things were not going well, as so often happened when

Harris met the media. Gallagher, who had a much more tolerant attitude to journalists than his boss, found himself repeatedly frowning as Harris did little to conceal his irritation at questions that he did not like, which tended to be most of them. Eventually, the press conference came to an acrimonious end and, after brusquely waving away further questions, a glowering Harris walked over to the Land Rover.

'Let's get out of here, Matty lad,' he said, swinging himself into the driver's seat. 'I've had enough of the media for one day.'

'You love them really,' said the sergeant as he joined his boss in the vehicle.

Harris grunted and began to reverse through the media scrum, cursing under his breath as a couple of journalists were slow to move out of the way, forcing him to hit the brakes to avoid hitting them.

'Try not to kill any of them,' said the sergeant. 'They can be useful, you know.'

'You sound like Curtis,' said Harris. The vehicle cleared the journalists and he started to guide it down the hill towards the western outskirts of the town. 'That's the kind of thing he's always saying.'

'Yes, well, he's right isn't he?' said the sergeant. 'Oh, don't give me one of your looks. The commander has got a point on this one.'

'What is this?' retorted the inspector testily. 'National Disagree With Jack Harris Day?'

'Of course not,' said the sergeant. He found himself choosing his words carefully with his boss for the second time in a matter of hours and tried to ease the tension that had pervaded the vehicle. 'All I'm saying is that we are going to need the journalists' help on this one and that means giving them as much information as we can. All you gave them was Carl Bradby's name and where the body was found.'

'What else should I have told them?'

'Well, you could have told them that he was ex-Army, and what he was doing on the Langdon Estate, but you didn't.'

'I have my reasons,' said Harris. 'I didn't mention the Dark Waters investigation because I don't want journalists pestering Stuart Liversedge until we've been able to talk to him first. And as for Bradby being ex-Army, it would not be long before they found out that he was mentioned in despatches and we'd end up with a media frenzy about a dead war hero. I don't want this to be investigation by media.'

Gallagher knew from experience that there was little to be gained by pressing the issue and opted instead to stay silent and stare out of the window as the outskirts of Levton Bridge gave way to moorland. He was relieved to see Harris's mood lighten after several miles as the inspector's beloved hills worked their magic on him, just as they always did, and conversation gradually returned to the vehicle. After a while, the Land Rover arrived at the M6, where it headed north into Scotland then turned west onto the A75 through Dumfries and Galloway. Eventually, Harris turned off and headed north towards the high peaks, swooping ridges and wooded slopes of the Galloway Hills. The detectives had entered Stuart Liversedge's world.

* * *

Back in the North Pennines, a team of detectives had spent a couple of hours re-interviewing staff members at the Langdon Estate. Alistair Marshall and Sally Orr sat down with Danny Brewster and Janice Garvey in the main office just after 3:00pm.

'I don't know what you expect us to say,' said Garvey. 'Like we keep telling you, we were having our lunch here at the time you think that poor man was murdered.'

'I know but sometimes people remember things,' said Marshall.

'There's not much to remember about sandwiches,' said Garvey with a slight smile.

'No, I suppose not,' said Marshall. 'I was thinking more of the man who died. Does anyone on the estate know Carl Bradby? Have you heard anyone mention his name?'

'I don't think so, I've certainly heard nothing,' said Garvey. She shook her head in disbelief. 'To think that something like that could happen here. Who would have thought it?'

Marshall looked at Danny Brewster.

'You're very quiet,' said the constable.

'He's still suffering from the shock of it all,' said Garvey.

'I appreciate that,' said Marshall. 'But I was–'

'I've told you everything!' exclaimed Brewster. 'Why won't you leave me alone?'

The door opened and office manager Miranda Jacobs walked into the room and glared at the detectives.

'What on earth is going on?' she demanded. She gave Brewster a concerned look. 'This is harassment and if it continues, I will ask Mr de la Roche to submit a formal complaint.'

Seeing little to be gained by further questioning, the detectives beat a tactical retreat and walked out into the yard where they met a worried Alison Butterfield.

'Problem?' asked Marshall.

'Yeah,' said Butterfield. 'I've looked everywhere but I can't find Ronny Carroll and no one seems to know where he is!'

Chapter nine

The light was beginning to fade when the detectives arrived at the Dark Waters wildlife rescue centre, alighted from the Land Rover and pushed their way through the main gate. As they did so, Harris noticed traces of red paint further along the fence. It looked recent, and although someone had tried hard to wipe it off, the words Say nothing could still be read.

'Clearly, all is not well in paradise,' said Gallagher. 'I am beginning to see why Liversedge was so cagey on the phone. It looks like he's got himself involved in something heavy.'

The detectives walked along the paved paths that took them past a ramshackle collection of aviaries, several of them containing small ponds. Waterfowl were everywhere, many of them bearing signs of injuries, and Harris paused on more than one occasion to look closer.

'That's a goosander,' he said, pointing at one bird in particular.

'Bit titchy for a goose, isn't it?'

'Ignoramus,' said Harris. 'It's a type of duck.'

'Whatever,' said the sergeant.

They continued walking until a whitewashed house came into view. As the detectives approached, the front door swung open and a man and a woman in their mid-to-late fifties emerged, silhouetted in the light from the hallway. Stuart Liversedge was a tall, wiry individual with a straggly black beard and thinning hair, dressed in jeans and a T-shirt, on the front of which was emblazoned the image of a swan. His wife was much smaller, had her brown hair tied back and was wearing a checked shirt and dungarees. The detectives could not fail to notice that, whereas Stuart looked composed, his wife came over as nervous; her eyes kept darting towards her husband, as if seeking reassurance from him. Harris glanced at Gallagher, who raised an eyebrow.

Once the introductions had been made, the officers followed Stuart Liversedge and his wife into the hallway of the house, which had a musty feel to it. Stuart noticed the sergeant wrinkle his nose.

'Damp,' he explained. 'We keep saying that we should get someone to take a look but we never quite get round to it. If you take the first door on the left, into the living room, we'll sort you some tea. You must be thirsty after your long journey, and Anna makes a mean macaroon, don't you, love?'

'So people tell me,' she said with a wan smile as she headed towards the back of the house. 'I'll bring everything through in a few minutes. You talk to them, Stuart.'

She disappeared into the kitchen and the detectives sensed that she was relieved to get away from them. Intrigued, the officers followed Stuart into the living room and sat down on a couple of threadbare armchairs, leaving their host to take his place on the equally worn sofa. Looking round the living room, Gallagher was struck by the fact that none of the furniture was new, not antique, just aged and shabby. Even the television standing on the rickety side table in the corner of the room was old and the sergeant doubted that it had access to many channels. The overall impression was one of neglect. Again, Stuart guessed what he was thinking and gave Gallagher a look that was almost apologetic, as if he had somehow let the sergeant down.

'You've probably worked out that we don't spend much on the house,' he said ruefully. 'Every penny that we bring in goes to fund our work.'

'When did you start Dark Waters?' asked Gallagher.

'When we moved here fifteen years ago. I managed a council transport department and Anna was an accountant but we'd got to the stage in our lives where we wanted to do something more worthwhile,' said Stuart. 'This was just the kind of place that we had been looking for. The old feller that owned it kept ducks so there were a couple of ponds already here and we have expanded over the years as people brought us more waifs and strays. You'll have seen them on the way in.'

'Very commendable,' said Gallagher.

'Anna's not as keen as I am,' said Stuart. 'She's been saying for a while that maybe we should get rid of the birds and move to somewhere a bit nearer civilisation.'

'I take it you don't agree?' said Gallagher.

'No, I love it here.'

'And the investigations?' asked the sergeant. 'How did they come about? They are a far cry from patching up a few injured ducks.'

'We fell into them by accident, really. Someone gave us a film of a couple of lads attacking mallards with catapults and we posted it on our Facebook page, not really thinking that much about it. The response was remarkable, more than two thousand people viewed it in the first month alone. After that, people kept approaching us with information so we started using some of our donations to hire our own investigators. Someone has to bring these people to book.'

Harris scowled and Stuart gave a wry smile.

'Your boss does not approve of our methods,' said Stuart. 'He does not like our attempts to name and shame wrongdoers because it shows up police failures.'

'Too true I don't,' said Harris. 'I would rather that you passed the tip-offs on to the police, not plaster them all over social media. You should let the professionals investigate these cases.'

'I will try not to be offended by that comment,' said Stuart. 'Besides, the police and other law enforcement organisations are free to make use of our material once it has been posted.'

'It's too late by then,' said Harris. 'The damage has been done. A friend of mine is a wildlife officer with North Yorkshire Police and tried to bring a case against a gamekeeper who your investigator filmed laying poison for birds of prey. The case collapsed when the estate's solicitor argued that there was no way he would receive a fair hearing, given that more than thirty-five thousand people had viewed the film.'

Stuart opened his mouth to argue the point but the inspector did not give him the chance.

'Anyway,' Harris said, 'we didn't come all this way to debate your methods. You said that we should be looking at another couple of people for Carl Bradby's murder?'

'You'll have heard of the River Caine? It runs through the hills not far from Ayr. Not that far from here, actually.'

'I read an article about it in a wildlife magazine,' said Harris. He shook his head. 'A tragic case.'

'What happened?' asked Gallagher.

'Someone dumped chemicals into the water,' said the inspector. 'Three times in a matter of weeks, as I recall. A lot of fish were killed.'

'*All* the fish were killed in the stretch of river that was affected,' said Stuart. 'Not to mention the likes of otters and kingfishers who fed on them. The Caine has not recovered and I suspect that it will be a long time before it does. To all intents and purposes, a ten-mile stretch of river is dead.'

'Very sad,' said Harris. 'But what's that got to do with our murder?'

'We hired Carl to investigate the incident,' said Stuart. 'We knew who was responsible right from the start. Everyone knows who did it, it's a case of getting hold of the proof.'

'And who *did* do it?' asked Harris.

'The Probert brothers. Graham and Jimmy. Have you heard of them?'

The detectives shook their heads and Stuart Liversedge was about to continue his explanation when there was a clinking sound and Anna walked into the room, carrying a laden tray, which she placed on the coffee table. She busied herself pouring the tea and handing round a plate of biscuits.

'I've just been telling them about the Proberts,' said Stuart.

Anna made as if to leave the room.

'Don't feel you have to go on our account,' said Harris. 'Feel free to stay.'

She shook her head.

'I'd rather not,' she said.

'Anna finds talking about the Proberts very upsetting,' explained Stuart. 'Don't you, love?'

She nodded and hurried from the room, tears glistening in her eyes. Harris waited for the door to close behind her.

'We saw the graffiti on your fence,' he said. 'Is that something to do with the Proberts?'

'It's part of their campaign of intimidation against us,' said Stuart. 'We've taken flak before, of course we have, it comes with the territory, but it's mainly been on social media. This is different. The brothers are determined to make sure that we drop our investigation.'

'And you think they are capable of murder, do you?' said Harris.

'Possibly,' said Stuart. 'They pretend to be respectable businessmen but it's all a front. They're a couple of out-and-out Glaswegian villains and nasty ones at that.'

'How come they have been dumping chemicals?' asked Harris.

'They run a waste disposal company out of an industrial estate on the outskirts of Glasgow. Kwikkie Waste Disposal. Their motto is "We worry so you don't have to", which is ironic, given that everyone who is unfortunate enough to cross their path ends up worrying like hell.'

'What kind of waste do they handle?' asked Gallagher.

'Anything they can get their hands on. The kind of stuff that would cost a fortune to move if you used a legitimate company. Their clients are mainly small businesses and they charge rock-bottom prices, which they achieve by cutting corners.'

'Like dumping stuff in the River Caine,' said Gallagher.

'And other waterways,' said Stuart. 'We know of at least four streams that they have used. The Caine is by far the most seriously damaged but they've all suffered to varying degrees.'

'It's truly wicked,' said Harris.

'You can see why we were so keen to take the case on when we were asked to investigate by a community group in one of the villages along the Caine. That was before we discovered what the Proberts were capable of.'

'The villagers knew that it was down to them, did they?' asked Gallagher.

'They did. An old dear from Lane End saw their truck heading for where the chemicals were dumped the third time it happened. The name on the side had been obscured but the cover had slipped.'

'Why did the villagers come to you?' asked Harris. 'Surely there are other organisations who could take on something liked that? The Scottish Environment Protection Agency? The water company? The police?'

'You know my views on how seriously the police take wildlife crime, Chief Inspector. Anyway, for the record, they went to the police first and, although there were several meetings between the various organisations, nothing happened. It didn't help that the old dear who saw the brothers' truck decided to withdraw her statement once she heard more about the Proberts. The villagers decided that we were the best option and we thought that Carl Bradby was the ideal person for the job, given his SAS training in covert surveillance.'

'Did he get the evidence you needed?' asked Gallagher.

'He followed them for several weeks and filmed them dumping chemicals in a stream near Ayr. That's when the intimidation began. They started driving slowly through the village then turned their attention to us. Then there was the graffiti at the front gate and silent late night phone calls and threatening anonymous letters. Anna's absolutely terrified. Wants us to leave this place.'

'I don't blame her,' said Gallagher. 'You're very isolated up here. I take it the film has been posted on your social media?'

'Not yet. Carl reckoned that they'd dump some more chemicals again pretty soon and he wanted to film that as well before we went public. He said the more evidence we had, the better. Then, when the intimidation started, Anna asked me not to put it up so I've just hung on to it.'

'If it's not gone public, how come the brothers know about your investigation?' asked Harris.

'I don't know. I haven't told them and I can't see anyone from the village talking to them either.' Stuart Liversedge frowned. 'Clearly, someone tipped them off, though. Anyway, you can see why I think there's a chance that the Proberts killed Carl, can't you? They're evil.'

Both detectives nodded in agreement.

'Did you not tell the local police about the intimidation?' asked Harris.

'They said that it would require a surveillance operation and they didn't have the spare manpower. However, now that it's a murder inquiry, they won't be able to ignore it, will they?'

'They certainly won't,' said Harris. He glanced at Gallagher. 'We need to talk to the local cops. Find out why the hell they didn't try harder to get the Proberts behind bars.'

Gallagher sighed quietly; he recognised a situation that required someone with deft political skills. Jack Harris may be many things, but diplomatic was not one of them. The inspector's ringing mobile phone disturbed his reverie.

'Gillian,' he said to Gallagher. He took the call but it cut out within seconds.

'I'd go outside to ring them back,' said Stuart. 'Reception is not very good in the house. I find that the best spot is next to the shelduck.'

When Harris had left the room, Stuart looked at Gallagher.

'Why did your boss mention the Anti-Fishing Alliance when I spoke to him earlier today?' he asked.

'Their name cropped up in our investigation into Carl Bradby's murder.'

'Do you think they had something to do with it?'

'We've heard nothing that makes us think that,' said Gallagher. 'Have you?'

'Nothing specific but I did hear that they are looking to expand the area in which they operate and it wouldn't surprise me if the Langdon Estate is on their radar. Sebastian de la Roche doesn't exactly keep his opinions to himself. I'm surprised they've not had a go at him already.'

'And there was me thinking that fishing was a nice, peaceful pastime,' said Gallagher.

'You have no idea,' replied Stuart.

The door opened and Harris walked back.

'Problem?' asked Gallagher, noting the grim expression on his face.

'The Proberts may have to wait,' said Harris. 'It would appear that Ronny Carroll has done a runner! You can say I told you so, if you want. I imagine everyone else will.'

'No, I think I'll leave that to Alison.'

Harris gave him a rueful look.

Chapter ten

The next morning found Jack Harris in Sebastian de la Roche's office, enduring a furious tirade from the owner of the Langdon Estate. La Roche had not even given the detective a chance to sit down before he began to angrily air his grievances about the fact that large numbers of uniformed officers had arrived that morning to continue their search of the site and its many offices and outbuildings.

'I have a good mind to submit an official complaint,' said La Roche. He jabbed an accusatory finger at Harris. 'Your officers are tramping all over the place like bloody elephants, not to mention upsetting my staff with their endless questions.'

Harris opened his mouth to respond but La Roche denied him the opportunity to speak.

'I wouldn't care if they were different questions,' said La Roche, 'but, as far as I can see, they keep asking the same ones time and time again. When will you get it into your thick skulls that my staff had nothing to do with Carl Bradby's death? And as for your treatment of young Danny Brewster, it's nothing short of disgraceful!'

Harris tried to reply yet again but still La Roche continued with his litany of complaints.

'To say nothing of Ronny Carroll,' he said. 'You've got absolutely nothing to prove that he was involved in the murder so why on earth do you keep saying that he is a suspect? If I were him, I'd sue you. No wonder he's made himself scarce. It's not good enough, it really isn't. It's damaging the estate's reputation and costing me money. I have already had two calls from groups wanting to cancel fishing days with us and I have no doubt that there will be more. We're all over the media and you can't move for photographers trespassing to get their pictures.'

La Roche's eyes narrowed as he looked at Harris.

'You've never liked me and if your intention is to drive me out of business, you're going the right way about it,' he said. 'We're the innocent victims in this and you would do well to remember it.'

'Yes, well, as for innocent,' said Harris, finally managing to get a word in, 'you might as well know that your estate has been under investigation for a couple of weeks.'

La Roche looked at him suspiciously.

'Under investigation?' he said. 'For what?'

'Setting snares for otters.'

'I knew that's what this was about!' exclaimed La Roche triumphantly. 'You have never forgiven me for suggesting that they are culled, have you? Well, there's plenty of anglers who would applaud me for what I believe. You should have seen the letters of support I received after I did that interview with the newspaper. And as for an investigation, surely you have better things to spend your time on?'

'We're not the ones doing the investigation,' said Harris.

'Then who is?'

'Carl Bradby was working for Dark Waters.'

'That bunch of troublemakers!' exclaimed the estate owner. His eyes narrowed as he looked suspiciously at the detective. 'How long have you known about this?'

'I've only just found out.'

'Had Bradby found anything?' asked La Roche, his anger subsiding to be replaced by unease.

'An otter that was killed by a snare set near one of your ponds. Dark Waters plan to post the story online.'

'Can't you tell them not to?'

'Why would I?' said Harris. 'It's between you and them.'

'Yes, well, all I can say is that they had better be careful who they accuse. I don't know who laid the snare and neither do any of my staff.'

'I don't believe that for a moment,' said Harris. 'And I am sure you can appreciate why I am so interested. Carl Bradby finds an otter in a snare that was probably set by your water bailiff and, lo and behold, the next thing we know he is murdered on your riverbank and Ronny does a vanishing act. Now, call me suspicious…'

The inspector did not complete the sentence; he did not need to. La Roche was becoming ever more aware of the situation in which he found himself.

'I'm sure Ronny wouldn't do anything like that,' he said.

'Come on, Sebastian, the man's got form,' said Harris. 'And as for my officers, they'll be here until we find out where he's hiding out. The sooner we satisfy ourselves that he is not on the estate, the sooner we can leave you in peace. Are you sure you don't know where he is? I'd hate to think that you have been holding out on us.'

'I hope you are not suggesting that I am somehow involved in what has happened?' said La Roche. 'I am a respectable businessman and to suggest that I had something to do with the death of Carl Bra–'

'I am not suggesting anything of the sort but Ronny *is* your employee, isn't he? And he does what you tell him to do, does he not?'

La Roche considered the comment for a few moments then nodded. He sensed that the time had come to strike a more conciliatory tone with the detective.

'I'm not stupid,' he said. 'I know what Ronny is like, but he told me that he had nothing to do with the murder and I believe him.'

'Well, if you hear from him, I want to be the first to know about it,' said Harris. 'Understood?'

La Roche gave him a bleak look and Harris left the office and walked out into the yard, where he was approached by Butterfield and Gallagher. The inspector sighed when he saw the young constable's efforts to avoid looking smug following the news that Carroll had disappeared.

'It would appear that our Mr Carroll is in the wind then,' said the inspector. 'Any luck tracking down his family?'

'The only one I can find is his brother,' said Butterfield. She tried hard to sound professional. 'But he hasn't seen Ronny since they had a big falling-out last Christmas.'

'What happened?'

'They'd been drinking and Ronny took exception to something Davie said about their mother. She'd only been dead a few months. Ronny broke his brother's nose and they haven't seen each other since.'

'Grief works in strange ways, does it not?' said Gallagher with a slight smile. 'Does Davie know where his brother might hide out?'

'If he does, he's not telling us,' said Butterfield. 'He said that he wants nothing more to do with Ronny.'

'A luxury I think that we would all appreciate,' said Harris. 'Does Davie know anyone else that we can talk to?'

'Ronny sometimes comes into Levton Bridge to drink at the pubs in the marketplace,' said the constable. 'I thought it might be worth me asking around.'

'Much good may it do you,' said Gallagher sourly. 'When I investigated that attack in The Golden Pheasant last year, everyone clammed up. Twenty-three people having a drink on a Friday night and none of them saw Ronny smash a beer glass into Joe's face. Remarkable.'

'And we're sure that Ronny does not have a mobile phone, are we?' asked Harris. 'Because if he has, we may be able to track him down that way.'

'He definitely does not use one,' said Butterfield. 'Or email, either. The office staff keep trying to get him to change but he's old school, is Ronny. Lives life pretty much off the grid.'

'Well, keep looking anyway,' said Harris.

Butterfield nodded and headed across the yard.

'She must be loving this,' said Harris when she was out of earshot.

'I'm sure the thought has never crossed her mind,' said Gallagher with the slightest of smiles.

'Oh, yeah, like that's true,' said Harris. He frowned. 'I know everyone fancies Ronny for this but the thing that keeps nagging away at me is how likely is it that a former SAS man like Carl Bradby, with all his training, would allow himself to be bested by a thug like Carroll? It just doesn't ring true, Matty lad. However, it might if he was confronted by more than one attacker, particularly if they were Glaswegian hard men with good reason to see him silenced.'

'Where are we with the Proberts?' asked Gallagher.

'I'm waiting for a call back from Police Scotland. Suffice to say that the DC I talked to on the phone last night knew all about them. They would appear to be notorious.'

'So, if they are that notorious, how come they have not been locked up?' asked Gallagher.

'Good question and the DC I talked to last night got pretty uptight when I asked him. I got the impression that it was a sore point.' The inspector's mobile phone rang. *Number Unknown*. 'Maybe this will shed some light on things.'

He took the call.

'Jack Harris,' he said. 'Who am I talking to, please?'

'DCI Maureen Strothers at Police Scotland,' said a woman in a voice that suggested that she was less than pleased to be talking to him. 'I understand that you are another of those smart-arses who wants to tell me how to do my job...?'

Chapter eleven

Maureen Strothers suggested that they meet at a motorway services on the northbound M74, halfway between the North Pennines and her base in Glasgow, and it was Harris's Land Rover that arrived first. After taking the dogs for a walk round the car park, he and Gallagher returned the animals to the vehicle and headed for the service station's main concourse, where they took their hot drinks to a corner table in the café. As he sat down, Gallagher glanced towards the entrance, the first of several such looks over the next five minutes.

'Relax, will you?' said Harris, taking a sip of his tea.

'I can't,' said the sergeant. 'I keep wondering what kind of a reception we'll get. I've lost count of the number of times you've got me into situations like this and I don't fancy a stand-up row with a grizzled Scottish DCI in the middle of a motorway service station.'

'I'm sure she'll be fine.'

'You can't blame her if she's not, though,' said Gallagher. 'We would not exactly welcome some cop we'd never heard of, ringing up out of the blue and demanding to know why we had not nicked one of our local villains, would we?'

A woman in her mid-thirties, smartly dressed in a black suit, with short dark hair and carrying a briefcase, entered the coffee house and looked round as if seeking someone.

'Do you reckon this is her?' asked the sergeant. The woman noticed that they were watching her, gave a cheery wave of recognition and start walking briskly towards them. 'No, it can't be.'

'Jack Harris?' asked the woman in a voice with a soft Scottish lilt as she arrived at the table.

'That's me,' said Harris. He stood up. 'You must be Maureen Strothers.'

'The grumpy one,' she said with a smile, as they shook hands.

'Matty Gallagher, ma'am,' said the sergeant, relieved that it looked as if a diplomatic incident had been avoided. 'Can I get you a cup of tea?'

'Chamomile, please,' said Strothers. She sat down and looked at Harris. 'You've brought him up well, Jack, he's a fine young man and a credit to you and his mother.'

Both detectives warmed instantly to her, and as Gallagher headed for the counter, he was still chuckling at the joke. Once the sergeant had gone, Strothers gave Harris a rueful look.

'I think that we got off on the wrong foot this morning,' she said. 'I wasn't in the best of moods. My superintendent was more of a pain in the proverbial than normal. Thirteen burglaries and a stabbing overnight and he thinks that I have time to read every line of the latest report from HR. It wasn't professional and I apologise.'

'We've all been there,' said Harris. 'I've been chewing the head off my lot. Unfortunately, I'm not in the best of positions to do that, since I am the one who let our main suspect slip through our fingers!'

'I thought the Probert brothers were your main suspects?'

'It's not that simple. I'll explain when Matty gets back.'

They made small talk for a few minutes until Gallagher returned with the tea and a packet of biscuits. Strothers nodded her thanks, took a sip of her drink, reached for a digestive then opened her briefcase and removed two police mugshots which she slid across the table.

'There they are, in all their glory,' she said. 'The Probert brothers.'

Each picture depicted a burly, shaven-headed man with a sullen expression on his face. The striking resemblance between them made it obvious that they were brothers and the only way to tell them apart was that one of them had a scar on his right cheek.

'I didn't realise that they were twins,' said Harris.

'You could be forgiven for thinking that they are,' said Strothers. 'But they're not. There's eighteen months between them. Jimmy – the one with the scar on his right cheek – he's the youngest. Graham's the brains of the operation, although that's not saying much. They're just a couple of bully boys, really, as good an argument for thinning out the gene pool as ever there was.'

'How did Jimmy get the scar?' asked Gallagher.

'A fight in a Glasgow pub. The guy caught him with a flick-knife. Jimmy put him through a plate-glass window for his troubles. Severed an artery in the guy's arm. He was lucky that the ambulance arrived as quickly as it did. And, before you say anything, no, the brothers didn't get sent away for it.' Strothers gave a half-smile. 'We've never managed to get them into a court, something your governor so kindly reminded my colleague about on the phone last night.'

'I apologise,' said Harris. 'It had been a long day.'

'Actually, you were right to ask the question,' said Strothers. 'It's the biggest regret of my career so far that we have not locked them up. The bar-room brawl was a case in point. Saturday night and a packed pub and nobody saw a thing.'

'Yeah, we've got a few like that,' said Gallagher, thinking back to his dealings with Ronny Carroll. 'But, if you haven't got the brothers into court, how come you've got their mugshots?'

'It was the nearest we got to having them locked up. They were taken when they were arrested following a road rage incident a few months after the fracas in the bar. A teenager out for a drive in his dad's car three days after passing his test cut up the brothers' truck on the outskirts of Glasgow. They forced him off the road and gave him a good beating. Had a woman walking her dog not found him when she did and called an ambulance, we could easily have been looking at a murder. The kid made a statement implicating the boys from his hospital bed but he withdrew it after the Proberts paid him a visit the day after he was allowed to go home. What makes you think that they might have murdered this Bradby fellow?'

'Stuart Liversedge from Dark Waters suggested them,' said Harris. 'Do you know him?'

'I do,' said Strothers. She did not seem impressed by mention of his name. 'But I'm not sure he's right. The brothers tend to restrict themselves to north of the border, Glasgow mainly. They're very much homeboys. What's Stuart's link with Bradby anyway?'

'Bradby's body was found on a country estate that Stuart Liversedge had hired him to investigate for wildlife crime,' said Harris. 'Stuart said that he also brought Bradby in to investigate the Proberts.'

'That makes a bit more sense,' said Strothers. 'We knew that Stuart had hired someone to look at the Proberts but he would not tell us who it was. All we knew was that he was ex-military. The first time I heard the name Carl Bradby was when he was mentioned on Sky News. I'd have made the connection myself if they had reported that he was working for Dark Waters but they didn't.'

'Mea culpa,' said the inspector. He glanced at Gallagher. 'I should have given more detail at the press conference.'

The sergeant gave a slight nod of acknowledgment but said nothing.

'No harm done, you're here now,' said Strothers. 'I assume that Stuart was pretty scathing about us?'

'He seems to think that you didn't take the allegation of dumping chemicals in the river seriously,' said Harris. 'How come it came to you anyway? I wouldn't have thought that it was your kind of thing.'

'It's not really but we were approached by the chairman of the community association in Lane End, one of the villages along the river. We'd investigated a burglary at their community centre. I said we'd do what we could to help because we've been after the brothers for years and I fixed up several meetings with our wildlife team, the Scottish Environment Protection Agency and the water company. I even offered to turn over a couple of officers to do some surveillance on the Proberts.'

'So why does Stuart think that you did not take it seriously?' asked Gallagher.

'Because we were not moving fast enough for him. We might have got there in the end but it's also entirely possible that we wouldn't because when my superintendent found out how involved we were, he was less than impressed. He kept banging on about the amount of overtime it would need and said that there were more important things on which to focus our resources. He doesn't care about wildlife crime. He's much more interested in burglaries.'

'Mine is more interested in quad bikes stolen from farms,' said Harris. 'I'm the wildlife liaison officer in my area but he's not that interested.

'Well, there you are,' said Strothers. 'Anyway, there was no way we had enough to justify a prosecution, I was coming under increasing pressure to drop it, and the next thing I know Dark Waters are involved, so my super instructed that we wait to see what they turned up. The other agencies agreed – they're all being squeezed on manpower.'

'What about the attempts to intimidate Stuart and his wife?' asked Harris. 'He reckons that the police did nothing about that either.'

'That's only just happened and I tried to explain to Stuart that I needed something definite to persuade my boss to sanction a major surveillance operation. I have rung him several times to check that they are OK but all I get is the answerphone and he never returns my messages. Had Carl Bradby come up with anything, do you know?'

'A film of the Proberts dumping chemicals in another stream,' said Harris.

'He's not posted it on their social media, has he?' said Strothers. She looked worried. 'That's all I need.'

'Not yet, he hasn't,' said Harris. 'And I doubt he will so long as his wife is so frightened. He may let the police have a look at it, I suppose, but my guess is he'll need a lot of persuading, particularly now there's a possibility that it cost Carl Bradby his life.'

'Well, we'll give you all the help we can, of course,' said Strothers. 'We have not exactly covered ourselves in glory on this one but now that it's a murder inquiry, my superintendent can't fob me off when I ask for more manpower. Maybe we can make amends. What's your next move? Talk to the Proberts?'

'I'd like to see the stretch of the Caine where the chemicals were dumped first. It'll give us a better feel for what's been happening.'

'I thought you might. The community association chairman at Lane End is happy to meet you. I think you'll like him. He's quite a character and not the type to be intimidated by a couple of yobs, even though he's well into his eighties…'

Chapter twelve

Harris and Gallagher stood on the riverbank and stared in sombre silence at the River Caine. On a first, cursory glance, there appeared to be little wrong as it snaked its way through the narrow wooded valley but as the detectives looked closer, it did not take long for the signs of the catastrophic damage caused by the chemicals to become clear. There was an unhealthy tinge to the water and nothing moved, no silver dart of fish, no plants rippling in the current, no insects skimming across the surface, and as the officers listened, the awful impact of the chemicals became even more pronounced; there was no sound on the riverbank, no buzzing of bees moving from flower to flower, no chatter of birdsong. Death had settled its hand on the upper reaches of the Caine.

Harris, who had left his dogs in the back of the Land Rover for fear of them encountering toxic chemical residue on the riverbank, shook his head in disbelief and glanced at Gallagher.

'I've never seen a dead river before,' said the sergeant in a quiet voice. 'Not even in the worst parts of the Thames when I was growing up. There was always something alive. You ever seen anything like this?'

'No, I haven't,' said Harris. The inspector looked beyond Gallagher, along the riverbank to a tall, elderly, white-haired man wearing a tweed jacket with a scar on his right cheek. He was clearly fighting strong emotions as he stared out across the water. 'The old man seems to be taking it hard.'

'I'm not surprised,' said Gallagher, looking at Gregor McAllister, the chairman of Lane End Community Association. 'It must be heartbreaking seeing something like this done to a place you love.'

The pensioner, who lived in a cottage a hundred metres away on the riverbank, had led the detectives to the spot where the last batch of chemicals had been poured into the water. A patch of dead, discoloured grass was testament to the act. McAllister noticed that the officers were looking at him and walked over to them. As he neared, they could see that his eyes glistened with tears.

'I'm sorry,' he said. He produced a handkerchief, with which he dabbed his eyes as he walked towards them. 'I still get upset.'

'Don't apologise,' said Harris. 'It's entirely understandable. What they did here was wicked.'

'It was,' said McAllister. He gave a heavy sigh. 'They just didn't care, that's the thing that gets to me. This used to be such a magical place before the chemicals were dumped and they destroyed it without a moment's thought. Are either of you fishermen?'

'I am,' said Harris.

'Well, then you'll realise the enormity of what they did. The river was full of trout. At the right time of year, you couldn't move for them but since the chemicals were dumped, there's been nothing. And, as for wildlife, you only had to stand here for a couple of minutes before you saw a kingfisher. We had a healthy population of water vole as well and we'd just started to enjoy regular sightings of otters. We thought that they might even have been breeding, the first time that had happened on the Caine for eighty-five years. Everyone was so excited.'

The old man gestured to the river.

'Now look at it,' he said in a voice that was laced with bitterness. 'God knows how long it will take it to recover. Assuming that it ever does.'

'How much of the river has been affected?' asked Gallagher.

'You can see the signs all the way downstream but the worst effects are spread over ten miles. The water company's sampling showed traces of hydrochloric and sulphuric acid, possibly from batteries. They found evidence of a number of metals and benzene as well.'

'What's benzene?' asked the sergeant.

'It's used in industrial manufacturing processes, including dyes, solvents, insecticides and some electronics. It's highly toxic.' McAllister gave a mirthless laugh. 'You see what an expert I've become, thanks to the Proberts? They should have been locked up for what they did.'

'You weren't impressed with the way the authorities handled things, I believe?' said Harris.

'I thought Maureen Strothers might be able to get something done but, although she is well-meaning enough, she did not seem to have the backing of her boss. All that changed when Dark Waters became involved. For the first time, we felt that we were not alone and Stuart made it clear that he was not prepared to let intimidation stop him from doing the right thing. Until the Proberts got to his wife, that is. And the news of Carl Bradby's death will not have helped, of course.'

'I sense that you are not the type of man to give in to intimidation, though,' said Harris.

'It takes more than a couple of bully boys to scare me.' McAllister pointed proudly to a badge pinned to his lapel.

Harris leaned forward to look closer.

'The King's Own Scottish Borderers,' he said.

'I was with them for fourteen years,' said McAllister. 'Korea, then Malaysia in '65. After what I saw there, the Proberts are nothing.'

'I was with the Army before I joined the police,' said Harris.

Gallagher stared in surprise at his boss. The inspector rarely spoke of his military career, particularly to people he did not know, and, even when he was persuaded to do so, it was reluctantly and only when he felt that he had no option. And he never volunteered the information.

'I thought I recognised something about your bearing,' said McAllister. 'Who were you with, might I ask? I am guessing the Paras, a lad of your build.'

'Correct in one. I served alongside some of your lads, as a matter of fact. You knew you could rely on them if you were in a tight spot.' Harris gave a slight smile. 'Particularly if things kicked off in the bar.'

'That sounds like them,' said McAllister. He returned the smile. 'How old were you when you enlisted?'

'Three weeks past my sixteenth birthday.'

'You were very young then.'

'Yeah, I fell in with a bad crowd and knew that I had to get away,' said Harris. 'If I hadn't joined the Army, I'm pretty sure that I'd have ended up in prison. A number of the lads I kicked around with did. The Army gave me an opportunity to put things right.'

Gallagher watched with growing amazement as his boss continued to volunteer information.

'Well, it clearly worked,' said McAllister. 'I'm not sure why Carl Bradby joined. As you have no doubt gathered, he was a very secretive man. Whenever he said anything about himself, you had the distinct impression that he felt he had gone too far and he would fall silent.'

'I didn't know that you had met him,' said Harris.

'Just the once. Stuart brought him to see me after he had hired him. We had afternoon tea at my cottage. Stuart says that you think the Proberts killed him. Is that right?'

'We'd rather not say,' said Harris. 'Not at this early stage in the investigation, anyway.'

'I won't tell anyone, if that's what you are worried about,' said McAllister. 'I was in Army Intelligence for a while. I know all about keeping secrets.'

'I'm sure you do,' said Harris. 'But for the moment, I am keeping an open mind.'

'For which read "not convinced",' said McAllister.

'There's not much gets past you, is there?' said Harris with a wry smile. 'Well, you're right, Gregor, I am far from sure that they killed him. What do you think?'

'I share your doubts, Chief Inspector. Even though I am sure that the Proberts are capable of murder – well, Jimmy certainly is – from what I saw of the SAS in Palestine, they knew how to look after themselves. Are we really saying that a couple of common or garden yobs like the Proberts would be capable of getting the better of a highly trained man like Carl Bradby?'

Harris pondered the comment for a few moments, struck once more by the old man's shrewdness. It was the question that the inspector kept coming back to, the one that had troubled him ever since he first saw Bradby's body lying on the riverbank, the reason that he was struggling to believe that either Ronny Carroll or the Probert brothers were responsible for the murder. Or, if it came to it, that a couple of wild-eyed animal rights activists could get the better of a former Special Forces man. He noticed the others looking expectantly at him, waiting for his reply.

'One thing is certain,' he said. 'Whoever killed him had a violent streak and that certainly fits the description we have been given of the brothers.'

'It does indeed,' said McAllister. 'But they're like all bullies, they do not like it when someone stands up to them. They certainly didn't when I told them to sling their hook.'

Harris gave the old man a sharp look.

'You did what?' he said.

'I told them to get lost.'

'When was this?' asked the inspector.

'They knocked on my door one evening a couple of weeks back and said that they knew that I had called in Dark Waters and that I had better keep my mouth shut if I knew what was good for me. After I told them to go away, they uttered a few threats and have not been back since. I don't imagine that they will. Like I say, men like that are cowards at heart.'

'I thought Maureen Strothers would have mentioned this?' said Harris, looking at Gallagher. 'I wonder why she didn't.'

'Because she didn't know,' said McAllister. 'I didn't tell her. Or Stuart, for that matter.'

'Why not?' asked Gallagher.

'The police don't seem particularly keen to do anything and Stuart's wife was already worried enough, what with everything that was happening, and I didn't want to add to her concerns. Besides, I may be getting on a bit, but I am perfectly capable of dealing with a couple of low-lifes like that without help from anyone else.'

'You're also in your eighties,' said Gallagher.

'Don't worry about me, gentlemen. Anyway, are you going to arrest the Proberts?'

'We would certainly like to talk to them,' said Harris. 'Quite what we can prove, I don't know, assuming that they did kill him, that is.'

'Well, whatever happens, I'm glad that someone is doing something,' said the old man. His eyes narrowed as he gazed out over the dead river. 'Someone needs to pay for what's been done here.'

'Amen to that,' said Harris.

The three of them walked in silence back along the riverbank and, as they approached the old man's cottage, the detectives were alarmed to see a young shaven-headed man standing on the front path, watching them suspiciously. McAllister noticed the detectives' expressions.

'Don't look so worried,' he said with a smile. 'Luke's my grandson. He lives with me. Rather like you, Chief Inspector, he got into trouble when he was a teenager and joined the Army. We hoped that it would straighten him out. It seemed to work for the first two or three years then he went off the rails again, got himself involved in a few drunken brawls and they kicked him out.'

McAllister smiled at Harris.

'It would appear that it doesn't work for everyone,' he said. 'Anyway, his parents asked me to take him in to see if it could help put him on the straight and narrow.'

'And did it?' asked Harris.

'It seems to have done,' said McAllister. 'He's got a job in one of the shops on the Forres Retail Park and he's had the same girlfriend for more than a year. And he's not been in trouble with the police since he left the Army.'

'Did he know about Carl Bradby?' asked Gallagher.

'He knew what Carl was doing but he didn't meet him.' McAllister noticed the detectives exchange glances. 'He's a trustworthy lad and he knew not to talk about it. The Proberts wouldn't have found out about us calling in Dark Waters from him.'

'Right,' said Harris.

McAllister opened the gate and they walked down the path to where Luke was standing, still eying the officers uneasily.

'Who's this, Grandad?' he asked.

'I am DCI Harris,' said the inspector. He held up his warrant card. 'This is DS Gallagher. We're based in Levton Bridge.'

'What are you doing here?'

'They are investigating Carl Bradby's murder,' said his grandfather. 'They want to know if the Proberts might have killed him.'

'Yes, well, we don't want to discuss that,' said Harris quickly; there was no way he was ready to trust Luke McAllister yet.

'I do hope that it's not anything to do with them,' said Luke. He looked at the old man. 'Didn't I tell you to steer clear of things like this, Grandad? What if they hear that you've been talking to the police? The last thing we want is them coming back.'

'You worry too much,' said McAllister.

Luke switched his attention to the detectives and concern replaced suspicion.

'I keep telling him that you can't be too careful when you're dealing with people like the Proberts,' he said. 'He seems to forget that he's not in Korea now but he won't listen.'

'Well, he should,' said Gallagher, looking at the pensioner. 'Your grandson is right, Gregor. You really do need to be careful.'

'I can look after myself,' said McAllister defiantly.

'Just listen to what he says,' said Harris.

Luke shot the inspector a grateful look then, with farewells completed and warning duly repeated to reiterate the point, the detectives walked back towards the inspector's Land Rover.

'Luke seems a decent kid,' said Gallagher.

Harris did not reply.

'I know that silence,' said the sergeant. 'I take it that you don't agree?'

'I'm not sure,' said Harris as they reached the vehicle and he opened the back up to be greeted enthusiastically by the dogs. 'There's something about him that doesn't feel quite right.'

'That's your suspicious mind,' said Gallagher as he got into the passenger seat. 'He seemed OK to me.'

Harris did not reply immediately but instead busied himself pouring water from a plastic bottle into a dish for the dogs then opening a bag of treats for the animals. He closed the back again and came round to the front of the vehicle.

'Sure, Luke may be a bit rough and ready,' said Gallagher, returning to his theme as his boss slid himself into the driver's seat, 'but he obviously cares a great deal for his grandfather. You seemed quite taken with the old man yourself, I think?'

Harris nodded but, before he could reply, his mobile phone rang. The inspector put the call on speaker when he saw that it was from Leckie.

'Now then,' said the intelligence officer. 'I've just texted you a link which you'll want to take a look at PDQ. I think that I may have a lead on your murderer.'

'Well, whoever it is, they'll have to get in the queue,' said Harris.

'No, don't thank me,' said Leckie.

Chapter thirteen

Jack Harris clicked on the link on his smartphone and placed the device on the dashboard of the Land Rover so that both he and Gallagher could see the website on the screen.

'You called it up yet?' asked Leckie's voice. 'It should take you to the Anti-Fishing Alliance website.'

'Got it,' said Harris. 'But I check it regularly and there's nothing there of much interest – campaign pieces, research, that kind of thing. Nothing to help us, really.'

'You just leave it to the professionals, son,' said Leckie. 'That's what you're supposed to think but our cyber people had begun to suspect that all that stuff was to give them a veneer of respectability and that there may be more to it than meets the eye – literally. Can you see that row of fish across the bottom of the home page? Click on the fifth one along, the one with the pinkish tinge.'

Harris did as instructed and a blank page appeared on the screen, at the top of which was a small panel asking him to fill in a number.

'The code changes every day and today's is *fishing4569*,' said Leckie. 'Key that in.'

Again, Harris did as instructed and this time a series of boxes appeared, each one bearing the image of a movie camera.

'What you are looking at,' said Leckie, 'is the private page for members of the alliance, the bit the general public doesn't see. If you click on the cameras, they call up different videos. This is how Miriam Coles and Guy Robertson communicate with their members and there's some pretty startling stuff. It explains why we are so interested in them.'

'How did you know to click on that particular fish and what code to use?' asked Gallagher. 'Have you got someone on the inside?'

'We keep getting anonymous tip-offs but have no idea who it is. Whoever it is, they know how to cover their tracks. Mobile calls we can't trace, disguised voices, no-reply emails, social media messages from fake account holders.'

'Just like the person leaking information from the Langdon Estate,' said Gallagher. 'There's a lot of stirring going on.'

'You're OK to click on any of the videos,' said Leckie. 'Our cyber guys say that no one can see who is visiting the page. Go for the one at the top left. It's just gone up.'

Harris clicked the button to activate the film, which revealed Miriam Coles standing on a stretch of riverbank that the Levton Bridge detectives recognised.

'That's just along from the Langdon Estate, isn't it?' said Gallagher, glancing at Harris.

'It is,' said Harris. 'It's a wonder that none of our people saw her when they were doing the search.'

'The Alliance are very careful,' said Leckie. 'It's how they've kept out of trouble for so long. It's very frustrating.'

The film jerked into life and the image wobbled slightly for a few moments before stabilising; the video had clearly not been taken by a professional. Once the image had settled, Coles took a few steps towards the camera.

'Miriam here with an important update,' she said. She stopped walking and gestured to the sunshine sparkling on the river. 'A truly beautiful place, I am sure you will agree, but like so many of our riverbanks, one that is blighted by the activities of thoughtless anglers.'

'Oh, change the record,' said Harris with a sigh.

Gallagher smiled and they could hear Leckie chuckling.

'I am standing,' continued Coles, 'close to the Langdon Estate, a few miles from Levton Bridge, in the North Pennines. As you know, we have had concerns about the actions of its sleazeball owner Sebastian de la Roche for a while now. You will, no doubt, recall that he is determined to see a cull of otters because he says they are threatening his fish stocks. It's another example of the ill-informed arguments that anglers use to justify their so-called sport.'

'I can see where this is going,' said Harris gloomily.

'Presumably, where it always goes?' said Gallagher.

Harris nodded and leaned closer to the smartphone in an attempt to make out what Coles was saying as a sudden gust of wind rustled the trees on the riverbank. The inspector turned up the volume.

'As I am sure you know, there has been a murder at the estate,' continued Coles. 'The body of Carl Bradby was discovered about a quarter of a mile away from where I am standing. What you will probably not know, however, because the police, in their wisdom, have not seen fit to tell you, is that Carl Bradby was carrying out an investigation into the estate on behalf of Dark Waters. Our relationship with Dark Waters is not always an easy one – they are not radical enough for us – but that is not to say that some of their work does not have value. We understand that this investigation was started following a tip-off that Sebastian de la Roche ordered his water bailiff to set illegal snares to catch otters near his new fish ponds. We have been told that Carl Bradby had secured film of a dead otter in a snare, an image which will shock members of the public when Dark Waters releases it. You should not be surprised that the police have not revealed any of this information to the media, given that the murder investigation is being led by none other than Detective Chief Inspector Jack Harris, of Levton Bridge CID, an arch public apologist for the sport. So much for the impartiality of our police service.'

'Cheeky cow,' muttered Harris.

'DCI Harris has also kept from you the fact that Carl Bradby is a former soldier, who was twice mentioned in despatches for gallantry in the service of his country,' continued Coles. 'The man is a war hero and deserves better than for his achievements to be ignored by the police. DCI Harris also served in the military but one can only assume that his record was not as impressive, hence he does not feel that he can bring himself to mention a decorated comrade. That tells you everything you need to know about the man.'

The inspector glared at the screen angrily but said nothing as Coles continued to address the camera.

'All in all,' she said, 'the police have taken a distinctly laissez faire approach to the whole incident. Carl Bradby gave his life so that you would know the truth about what has happened here and we understand that the police in Levton Bridge have a strong suspect for his murder, namely, the water bailiff Ronny Carroll. However, he has not even been questioned and remains at large. This has caused, we have been told, considerable consternation among members of *Defective* Chief Inspector Harris's team.'

'A cheap jibe,' said Harris with a scowl.

'It is,' said Gallagher, 'but someone is clearly keeping her up to date with events on the Langdon Estate. I do hope it's not one of our people.'

'Whoever it is, there are too many people playing games,' said Harris as Miriam Coles continued her address.

'Ronny Carroll,' she said, 'is notorious for his violent behaviour and is believed to have carried out a number of serious assaults on people trespassing on the riverbank at the Langdon Estate in recent months, attacks that were carried out, we believe, at the loathsome Mr de la Roche's behest. However, no one has been charged in connection with any the assaults, for reasons known only to the police.'

'Because no one would sign a witness statement,' exclaimed Gallagher; it was his turn to be angry. 'It wasn't for want of trying.'

'There is also good reason to believe that it was Sebastian de la Roche who instructed Ronny to carry out the murder of Carl Bradby,' continued Coles. 'DCI Harris could easily have ordered the arrest of both men but one can only assume that his much-vaunted championing of wildlife pales into insignificance when compared with his slavish support for the angling industry. Oddly enough, the man himself has been remarkably elusive at a time when he should be keeping people informed. Jack Harris is guilty of a gross dereliction of duty and the people he purports to serve deserve better.'

'This is ridiculous!' exclaimed Harris. His eyes flashed fury. 'They're twisting everything I say. And we have never suggested that La Roche ordered the murder!'

'The result of all this, I suspect,' said Coles, 'is that, as you listen to me, you will find yourselves becoming increasingly angry and as you know, the AFA does not believe that we should stand aside at moments like this. We believe in direct action against men like Sebastian de la Roche and his brutish henchman Ronny Carroll, and that is exactly what we will do. I'll update you on our plans in the next day or so. Watch this space and keep the faith!'

The film ended and the image of the camera returned.

'Keep the faith!' said Harris with a snort of derision.

'The words "pigeons" and "cat" come readily to mind,' said Leckie's voice across the airwaves. If they go public with that little lot, there'll be hell on.'

'What do you think she means by "direct action"?' asked Gallagher.

'Well, if their past activities are anything to go by, it could be anything from arson to assault,' said Leckie. 'Whatever it is, it's likely to be violent. I would not want to be in Sebastian de la Roche or Ronny Carroll's shoes.'

With the conversation at an end, Harris phoned Gillian Roberts to update her on what had been happening.

'That's all we need,' she said. 'A bunch of lunatics running round our patch, hell-bent on revenge. Where do you think they're getting their information from, Jack? Hopefully, not one of our people?'

'I do hope not.'

'I'll keep my ear to the ground anyway,' said Roberts. 'What's our next move then?'

'I'm not sure we can do much until we see what Miriam comes up with. It sounds like we may have a bit of time in hand.'

'Are you on your way back?'

'No, we're going to stay the night in Glasgow. We'll not be back until tomorrow.'

'Well, if I might offer a word to the wise,' said Roberts, 'don't hang on up there any longer than you need to. Curtis keeps asking why you're not here. The Press Office has been besieged with calls from the media and he's getting jumpy because he has nothing to give them.'

'He's not the only one,' said Harris with a sigh. 'Can you update him on the state of play with the AFA, please? Not for public consumption but just so that he knows. Oh, and can you make sure that Sebastian de la Roche knows what's happening as well? I take it that there's no news on Ronny Carroll?'

'No, he's still in the wind,' said Roberts. 'I know you think these Glasgow guys are worth looking at, but my money is still on Ronny.'

'Yeah, me, too,' said Gallagher, speaking almost without realising that he had said anything.

A sharp look from Harris had Gallagher immediately regretting the comment as, having ended the call, his boss looked intently at his sergeant.

'So, you think we're wasting our time coming up here as well, do you?' he asked.

'I've made no secret of my views on Ronny Carroll.'

'True enough, but do the views of Stuart Liversedge not count for something as well? He's closer to this than we are and, surely, we have to take it seriously when he points us in the direction of the Proberts?'

'Obviously, we have to listen to him,' said Gallagher, trying to buy himself a few moments to seek the right words so as not to irritate his boss. 'But, on the other hand, there *may* be an argument for saying that Curtis is right and that we should be back at Levton Bridge, particularly if it's all about to kick off. Maybe we have allowed ourselves to be distracted by the Proberts because we are angry about what they have done to the rivers.'

'*We* or *me*?' asked Harris pointedly.

Gallagher did not reply, hoping that his silence would defuse the tension in the vehicle. It didn't and they left the village and travelled towards Glasgow in silence for a few minutes before Harris gave his sergeant a rueful look.

'You're right, of course,' he said. 'I have made mistakes on this one and it's time that I admitted it.'

Gallagher looked at his boss in surprise; humility had never been one of the personality traits of a man who had a strong faith in his own judgement and rarely confessed to having got something wrong, mainly because he rarely did. The sergeant was not quite sure how to respond.

'Well, it's a complicated situation,' he said. He tried to sound conciliatory. 'It's difficult to work out what's for the best.'

'It's kind of you to say so, Matty lad, but it isn't difficult, is it? I should have listened to what you and everyone else was saying. We should have brought Ronny Carroll in for questioning right at the start. As for the Proberts, they've probably got nothing to do with Carl Bradby's death but we still owe it to him to make sure, don't we?'

Gallagher nodded.

'You're right, of course,' he said. 'So what's the plan then?'

'We go and see Maureen for a chat now, as arranged, get her view on bringing in the Proberts and head back to Levton Bridge tomorrow. It doesn't sound like the AFA is going to do anything tonight and the DI is perfectly capable of handling whatever happens if they do.'

'Fair enough,' said Gallagher.

Further confrontation had been avoided and that was good enough for him.

Chapter fourteen

Strothers had booked Harris and Gallagher into a hotel on the edge of Glasgow and, having left their bags in their rooms, they made their way to a nearby police station where they were surprised to see that the DCI had much more in mind than a chat. Two dozen officers, some of them from the firearms unit, had gathered for a briefing about bringing in the Proberts for questioning and there was an atmosphere of eager anticipation. Noticing the look of surprise on the faces of the Levton Bridge detectives, Strothers had explained, 'Guilty or not, I wasn't going to miss an opportunity to ruin the brothers' evening!'

The briefing proved to be of benefit to Harris and Gallagher; it was a welcome opportunity to focus on solid police work and banish uneasy thoughts about their earlier disagreements. With the event having finished and a time of 9:00pm agreed for the raid, Harris took the dogs for a quick walk around a nearby park reserve then joined Strothers and Gallagher in the DCI's office, where, acutely aware that they had not eaten for many hours, they had ordered takeaway pizzas washed down with bottled beer. As they did so, the dogs eagerly eyed the inspector's meal and, occasionally, Harris would tear them off pieces.

'What did you make of Gregor McAllister, then?' asked Strothers. She reached for a slice of pizza. 'He's a remarkable man, is he not?'

'He certainly is,' said Harris. 'And he doesn't seem to be fazed by the fact that the Proberts called at his home.'

'They did what?' exclaimed Strothers.

'They turned up on his doorstep one evening and told him to keep his mouth shut.'

'Why does no one tell me these things?' said Strothers with a sigh. 'Why do I have to find out about it from you?'

'Gregor said that you didn't seem that interested in what was happening,' said Harris. 'I'm sure he's wrong.'

'Too right he is,' said Strothers vehemently. She was, clearly, upset by the comment. 'It's so galling that they should think I would ignore an old man being threatened on his doorstep by a couple of hoodlums. What did he do when the brothers turned up?'

'Told them to sling their hook.'

'He's too confident for his own good sometimes,' said Strothers with a shake of the head. 'I keep telling him that this is not Korea.'

'His grandson made the same comment,' said Harris. 'Do I assume that it relates to something in the Korean War?'

'Yes,' said Strothers. 'Our Gregor won the Military Cross.'

'I knew there was something about him,' said Harris, recalling how he had been impressed by the old man's bearing. 'What happened?'

'It's an amazing story,' said Strothers. The irritation of a few moments before had been replaced by her undisguised admiration for Gregor McAllister. 'Not that you'll ever hear it from him. I only found out about it because one of the villagers told me and, even then, I had to find out most of the details online. Gregor changed the subject when I asked him about it. His unit came under heavy fire trying to take a hill from the Chinese and his commanding officer was killed so Gregor took over. He ran at the enemy soldiers, throwing grenades, and the hill was taken. Did you see the scar on his face?'

The detectives nodded.

'That's when he was wounded,' said Strothers. 'A bullet shattered his cheekbone. I'm always struck by the fact that Jimmy Probert has a similar scar but that his was gained in a pub brawl. Says it all, really.'

'It certainly does,' said Gallagher. 'Gregor described the Proberts as cowards.'

'That's what worries me,' said Strothers. 'He lets his mouth run off and doesn't care who is listening. He forgets that he is not a young man anymore and that characters like the Proberts can be extremely dangerous if you get on the wrong side of them. You'll have noticed that we had our firearms people in the briefing tonight?'

'I did wonder why they were there,' said Harris.

'They were there because our intelligence guys picked up a rumour that Jimmy has recently taken to keeping a shotgun under the driver's seat of their truck. I keep telling Gregor that he has to be careful when dealing with the Proberts but I don't know how much notice he takes.'

'Not much, if his grandson is to be believed,' said Harris. 'Actually, I wanted to ask you about Luke. I was—'

He did not have chance to finish the sentence because Strothers' mobile rang and she picked the device up from the table.

'One of our surveillance teams,' she said. She put the call on speaker so that the others could hear. 'Helen, what's happening? Is Graham still at their yard?'

'Yes, and Jimmy's just arrived and they've left together in the truck,' said Detective Constable Helen Moore. 'We're wondering if they're up to their old tricks dumping chemicals. They've covered the company name on the side of the vehicle and we've checked the plates they've got on and they're fake.'

'Sounds like they could well be,' said Strothers. 'Keep me posted?'

'Sure,' said Moore.

Strothers ended the call and looked at the Levton Bridge detectives.

'Surely, the gods cannot be this kind to us, can they?' she said and made a call on her mobile. 'Phil, it's Maureen. Looks like we're going in a bit early. Is everyone ready? Good. I'll let you know.'

She placed her mobile back on the table.

'Between us, we'll get the scumbags for something,' she said cheerfully. She reached for another slice of pizza. 'Best eat this while we can. You were asking about Gregor's grandson, Jack?'

'Yeah, I was wondering what you make of him. Matty thinks he may be alright but I'm not sure.'

'I felt the same as you,' said Strothers. 'So, I did a bit of checking up on him.'

Harris nodded his approval.

'You find out anything interesting?' he asked.

'Nothing to worry me. After he was kicked out of the Army, he drifted from job to job, never lasting long at any of them, and picking up a string of theft convictions on the way. The last time he appeared in court was just over a year ago, when the magistrate warned him that, if he appeared before her again, he could expect to be sent to prison. That's when Luke moved in with Gregor. Gregor is too much of a gentleman to say it, but I sense that Luke had been a great disappointment. As I understand it, the lad's parents hoped that living with the old man might straighten him out.'

'Gregor seemed to suggest that it might be working,' said Gallagher, seeking anything that might vindicate the opinion of Luke that he had voiced earlier in the day.

'It would seem to be,' said Strothers. 'He's not been in trouble and Gregor says he's got a job in a shop. Speak as you find, the lad's devotion to his grandfather seems genuine. So, I guess in a way, both of you are right about him. A troublemaker going straight.'

Harris, who knew what Gallagher was thinking, gave him a wink. Gallagher smiled back; he appreciated the gesture at the end of a day in which there had been so much tension between the two men. Strothers' mobile rang again and she put it on speaker.

'Me again,' said Helen Moore. 'Something's definitely happening, ma'am. The truck has stopped at one of the manufacturing units at the Beech Road Industrial Estate and picked up three metal drums.'

'Excellent,' said Strothers. 'I'll get things moving at this end, you stick with the truck. Make sure that they don't clock you.'

She ended the call and gave the Levton Bridge detectives a triumphant look.

'Looks like we're on, gentlemen,' she said. She noticed that there was a little beer left in her bottle, swilled it and lifted it to her lips. 'Cheers!'

Chapter fifteen

'This is all Jack Harris's fault!' exclaimed Sebastian de la Roche as he stood in the living room of his house on the Langdon Estate and glared furiously at Gillian Roberts.

'I'm not sure that's fair,' said the detective inspector wearily; it had been a long day and it did not look like it was going to end anytime soon. She was not in the mood for another argument with the estate owner. 'He wouldn't–'

'I told him not to name us when he was talking to the media,' interrupted La Roche. 'But would he listen? Would he hell as like! First of all, we had bloody press photographers all over the place and now you tell me that I am being threatened by the crazies from the Anti-Fishing Alliance because they have got it into their heads that I am the kind of person who would order a murder. As if things weren't bad enough with Dark Waters and their meddling ways.'

'Yes, but I don't think it's fair to blame Jack for–'

'Of course it's fair to blame him! If he had not gone public about where the body was found, none of this would have happened.' La Roche gave her a suspicious look. 'Where is he anyway? I'm not impressed that he sends one of his lackeys to see me at a time like this.'

'Lackey?' said Roberts in a cold, clipped tone of voice.

'You know what I mean.'

'Yes, I do,' said the detective inspector. She gave him a hard look. 'And I don't appreciate it.'

'And exactly how long have you known about this anyway?' asked La Roche suspiciously.

'We received the information earlier today.'

'But you waited until mid-evening to tell me?'

'I've been busy,' said Roberts. 'Look, Sebastian, I came here out of the goodness of my heart to tell you that the Anti-Fishing Alliance is planning some kind of action against you. I would much rather be at home with my family.'

'Yes, well, at least I know where I stand on your list of priorities.' La Roche gave her an accusing look. 'It's a good job the AFA didn't decide to do something today, isn't it? And where *is* Jack Harris anyway? Too scared to face me?'

'I think you'll find that Jack Harris does not do scared,' said Roberts. 'For your information, he is pursuing inquiries outside the area.'

'Hopefully, he's gone to arrest the lunatics from the Anti-Fishing Alliance. They've got away with far too much, if you ask me, and now they are going round saying that me and Ronny are murderers. That's slander and they have already cost me money with their wild talk. They are the reason I had to take Danny Brewster on.'

'What do you mean?'

'We received a lot of online abuse after I gave a newspaper interview in which I suggested that otters be culled. I needed someone to help me manage it. Jack Harris did not exactly help. He appeared in the newspaper, saying that people like me did not understand the countryside and that made things ten times worse. People like him don't think of things like that when they make their grand pronouncements.'

'I take it that the abuse has continued?'

'Of course it has! Danny managed to block the worst offenders but stuff still gets through and it's been really bad since the murder was reported in the media. It's vile stuff, these people are sick, and what worries me is that Guy Robertson and Miriam Coles have moved beyond words and on to violence. You know those two fishermen who were attacked near Manchester?'

Roberts nodded.

'One of them was a good pal of mine,' said La Roche. 'He's lucky that they didn't kill him. You should have seen his injuries. He'll be scarred for life. The AFA are off their heads and the last thing I want is them trying it on with us.'

'Yes, well, you can be assured that we are taking their threat against you seriously. Have you seen anyone suspicious here over the past day or so?'

'Apart from all your police officers tramping all over the place?' said the estate owner; his brief moment of vulnerability replaced once again by anger. 'There were plenty of them, alright.'

'I was thinking more along the lines of animal rights protestors,' said Roberts. 'And might I suggest that if you want our help, you treat the police with a bit more respect?'

'Only if you earn it. If you want to put things right, you can start by protecting me and my family. I take it there will be police officers here tonight?'

'A minute ago, you couldn't get rid of us fast enough.'

'Yes, well that was before you told me that those loonies had threatened me,' said La Roche. '*Will* there be anyone here?'

'I am afraid we do not have the manpower to give you a guard.'

'You found enough people to keep an eye on the place after the murder,' said La Roche peevishly.

'That was because the forensics people had not completed their search of the area.'

'And I'm not as important, eh? Even if I end up getting injured – or worse? It hardly inspires confidence, Inspector.'

Roberts was about to issue a retort when she remembered the divisional commander's last words before she left Levton Bridge Police Station earlier that evening. 'Just remember,' Philip Curtis had cautioned her, 'Sebastian de la Roche is a victim until we can prove otherwise so I expect him to be treated as such. Get this wrong and it could turn into a public relations disaster.'

'If you need assistance tonight, ring 999,' she said, standing up and heading for the door. 'We'll respond immediately.'

'Yes, but how long will it take you to get here? We could have been murdered in our beds by the time your lot finally turn up.' La Roche's air of vulnerability had returned. 'I'm frightened, damn it. You've seen what these people are capable of doing.'

Roberts surveyed him for a few moments. His distress certainly appeared to be genuine so she tried to adopt a more empathetic approach; the last thing she wanted was to be the subject of an official complaint.

'I promise you that we'll be there as quickly as possible,' she said. 'And if the control room tries to fob you off, mention my name.If it helps, we are pretty sure that nothing will happen tonight.'

La Roche seemed to sense that there was little to be achieved by pursuing the argument any further so he followed the detective inspector into the hallway. As she opened the front door and stepped out into the night, she noticed that there was a light on in the office on the far side of the yard. 'Someone's working late.'

'Young Danny. I do not know what I would do without him. I said he could work from home but he said he would rather do it here.'

'Do you mind if I have a word with him before I go? Just in case there's something come in that might interest us?'

'You'll talk to him, regardless of whether I like it or not,' said La Roche. 'My wishes clearly count for nothing.'

'You don't help yourself, you know,' said Roberts. Complaint or not, she had had enough of the estate owner's truculence for one day and adopted her best matronly tone of voice. 'You really don't.'

La Roche took one look at the detective inspector's stern expression and decided not to engage any further with her and instead stood and watched in brooding silence as she walked across the yard.

Danny Brewster looked up anxiously from his laptop as she entered the office and sat down opposite him at the desk.

'Don't worry, you're not in trouble,' said Roberts. She nodded at the laptop. 'I see that your boss has got you working late.'

'You gotta work late when it comes to social media.'

'I imagine you do. I try to avoid it.' The detective inspector gave him a wry smile. 'I'm sure that he's paying you overtime. Or is it all out of the goodness of your heart?'

'Something like that,' said Brewster ruefully.

'Have you received anything on social media that might interest us?' asked the detective inspector.

'Like what?'

'Threats maybe? From the Anti-Fishing Alliance, perhaps?'

It seemed to the detective that the teenager stiffened slightly at the mention of the name.

'Do I take it that they *have* sent something?' she asked.

'They haven't, no.'

'Are you sure?'

Roberts stood up and made as if to walk behind him to look at the laptop's screen over his shoulder but he closed the device up.

'What are you hiding from me, Danny?' asked Roberts.

'Nothing. Honest. Besides, sending messages over social media isn't the AFA's style. If they're going to do something, they do it instead of talking about it.'

'How come you know how they think?' she asked, sitting down again. 'Do you know people who are members of the group?'

The teenager shook his head.

'You just get to hear things,' he said.

'What things, Danny?'

Brewster shook his head again, slid his laptop into his haversack and stood up. Clearly, thought the detective, the teenager did not intend to continue the conversation a second longer than he had to. She wondered whether to get heavy with him, compel him to stay until he had given proper answers to her questions, threaten him with a trip to the police station for further questioning. However, recalling the commander's words and feeling suddenly weary anyway, she decided that there was little to be gained from such an approach. There would be plenty of time to delve into Danny Brewster's background the following day, if need be.

'Are you OK to get home?' she asked.

'Yeah, I've got my motorbike.'

'Well, drive carefully,' said Roberts. 'It's been a long day and you'll be tired.'

'I'll be alright,' he said.

As they left the office, Brewster snapped off the office light behind her, plunging them into darkness and Roberts found herself surprised by a sudden wave of panic. It did not last long as the teenager immediately pressed another switch and light flooded the corridor once more.

'Sorry,' he said, 'didn't realise it was off.'

Something about the incident stayed with the detective inspector long after she had left the estate and was driving back to Levton Bridge.

Chapter sixteen

The Proberts' truck left Glasgow shortly after 9:15pm and travelled for the best part of an hour along country roads, all the time followed by unmarked police surveillance cars, whose drivers regularly switched their order to reduce the chance of detection. Their efforts were assisted by heavier-than-usual mid-evening traffic, which meant that their vehicles were less noticeable. However, maintaining the deception became more difficult on the country roads as the clock hands clicked past 10:00pm and the traffic thinned out. Eventually, the road was deserted apart from the truck and its constant companions, which were now hanging well back. Eventually, the lorry turned off onto a narrow lane.

'Bastards,' said Strothers, who was driving her own car with Harris in the passenger seat and Gallagher in the back; the dogs had been left in the care of a sergeant at the police station.

'What's wrong?' asked Harris.

'I have this awful feeling that I know where they are going. There's a small river about five miles down the lane, well, it's more of a stream really. It feeds into the Caine further downstream. My grandad used to take me and my sister there for picnics when we were kids. It's a beautiful spot. Ideal for sticklebacks and it's exactly the type of place the brothers like to dump their chemicals. They just don't care.'

Strothers slowed the car as they reached the side road and she and the other drivers in the police convoy sat with their engines running and lights dimmed for a few more moments as the truck disappeared into the distance until the only sign of it was a pinprick of light. To the officers' relief, the clouds parted to reveal a full moon, which made it a little easier to keep the vehicle in view.

'Don't let them get too far ahead,' said Harris, a sense of urgency in his voice. 'We don't want them poisoning it before we get there.'

Strothers nodded and led the convoy onto the side road, continuing to drive slowly.

'They've turned off,' said Gallagher.

The truck appeared to be making its way across open fields and within a minute, Strothers' car arrived at a gate that had been opened to reveal a rough track. The inspector extinguished the headlights and cut the engine and the other cars in the convoy did the same.

'We should walk from here,' she said in a low voice, opening her door. 'Less chance of giving ourselves away, and the stream is not far.'

The firearms team swiftly assembled their weapons and, acutely conscious that they could not hear the truck's engine and that every passing second increased the chance of another chemical incident, the officers half-walked, half-jogged down the track. They soon approached a copse and saw, glimpsed through the trees and illuminated by the truck's headlights, the spectral shape of the brothers unloading the metal drums and rolling them towards the water's edge. Strothers gestured to the sergeant who was in charge of the firearms team and he led them swiftly through the copse to emerge onto the riverbank just as

Jimmy unscrewed the lid of the first drum and his brother tipped it up, ready to pour.

'Police firearms officers!' shouted the sergeant. 'Put the drum down and get down on the floor!'

The brothers stared in horror at the weapons pointing in their direction. Graham slowly lowered the drum back to the ground, held up his hands in surrender and lay down as instructed but his brother hesitated.

'You!' shouted the sergeant. 'Hands where I can see them and get down on the floor!'

Still, Jimmy hesitated.

'Do what he says!' shouted Graham.

Still, his brother did not comply.

'Don't do anything stupid!' shouted the sergeant. 'We *will* open fire if we have to!'

Jimmy dived towards the truck, wrenched open the passenger side door and reached down into the well of the cab to emerge with his gun, but before he could use it, a shot rang out and he shrieked, dropped the weapon and staggered backwards, colliding with the truck. He sank to his knees and leaned against the vehicle, whimpering and clutching his right forearm, from which blood was already spurting. A couple of firearms officers darted forwards, one of whom grabbed the shotgun. Strothers walked over and looked down at the injured dispassionately as he fought back tears of pain.

'He told you not to do anything stupid, Jimmy,' she said. 'You've only got yourself to blame.'

Jimmy looked up balefully at her but, before he could issue a retort, the firearms officers hauled him roughly to his feet.

'I've called for an ambulance,' said Helen Moore. 'They say it could be twenty-five minutes, though.'

Jimmy groaned.

'Will he be alright?' asked Graham anxiously. 'Shouldn't you take him to hospital yourselves, if it's going to be twenty-five minutes?'

'It's a pity you never showed this much concern for your victims,' said Strothers. 'And since you ask, the car has just been valeted and I don't want to get blood on the seats.'

Gallagher glanced at Harris and raised an eyebrow. The inspector, for his part, smiled; he liked what he was seeing. Jimmy had heard Strothers' comment as well and gave her a foul look. However, before he could speak, one of the firearms officers began to administer first aid to his arm and he squealed in pain again, the last of the colour drained from his face and his breathing started to come more rapidly. Strothers continued to view his plight without emotion and turned her attention to Graham.

'What's in the drums?' she asked.

He did not reply.

'Well, we'll find out soon enough,' said Strothers. She gestured at Harris and Gallagher. 'And just to let you know, once I've finished asking you about the chemicals, these gentlemen have travelled up from Levton Bridge to talk to the two of you about a little matter of murder.'

'Murder?' said Graham. He looked genuinely surprised. 'What murder?'

'Carl Bradby,' said Harris.

'Never heard of him,' said Graham. He glanced at his brother with a look of feigned innocence. 'Have we?'

Jimmy clenched his teeth and shook his head.

'We'll see,' said Harris.

Twenty minutes later, headlights on the far side of the copse announced the arrival of the ambulance. Graham looked at his brother, who was calmer now, his breathing more controlled.

'I want to go the hospital with him,' he said.

'I don't think so,' said Strothers.

'Hang on a minute...' protested Graham.

Strothers gestured to one of the detectives.

'Phil,' she said, 'will you take Mr Probert back to the station, please? Hold him until I get there to see him booked in.'

Strothers watched as the protesting brother was led to one of the police vehicles. Before he got into the back seat, Graham gestured to her and she walked over to the vehicle and had an intense conversation with him for a couple of minutes before the car departed.

'What was that about?' asked Harris as she walked over to the Levton Bridge detectives.

'He wanted me to tell you that he's sticking to his story that he does not know your dead guy and that Jimmy will say the same.'

'They're probably right,' said Harris.

Chapter seventeen

The next morning, it was with some difficulty that Harris and Gallagher dragged themselves out of bed, after grabbing several hours of disturbed sleep. The inspector walked Scoot and Archie around a nature reserve close to the hotel then the detectives had breakfast before making their way into Glasgow, still feeling thick-headed and bleary-eyed when they arrived at the police station.

On arrival, Harris headed for Maureen Strothers' office; he had accepted her invitation to join her in the questioning of Graham Probert, the inspector telling Gallagher that he had done so more in hope than expectation. Gallagher took the dogs to the CID squad room where the detectives made a fuss of them and the sergeant sat down at a vacant desk next to the one occupied by Helen Moore.

'Do I take it that you'll be heading back after they finish interviewing Graham?' she asked.

'I reckon.'

The constable walked over to him and placed a couple of sheets of paper on the desk.

'Before you go, I'd be interested to hear your take on this,' she said. 'It's just come in.'

'What is it?' asked Gallagher, reaching for the document.

'A list of recent calls on Graham Probert's mobile. I think you'll find it interesting, even though it doesn't really help with your inquiry. It certainly opens things up for ours, I would suggest.'

Gallagher looked down the list of numbers. Moore had used a yellow marker pen to highlight an incoming one which appeared several times and had scrawled a name on the side of the page.

'Are you sure that's correct?' asked Gallagher.

'I am, and it poses a few questions, does it not?'

'Like why would Luke McAllister keep ringing the Proberts?' said Gallagher. 'You'd think they were the last people he would want to talk to. I suppose he could have been warning the brothers off. Telling them to stay away from his grandfather. He's very protective of the old fella.'

'That was my first thought but the fact that he made a number of calls to them looks more like he has some sort of relationship with the brothers. What do you think?'

'It does. That will make my governor feel a bit better. He was suspicious about Luke right from the start.' The sergeant gestured to another piece of paper lying on the constable's desk. 'What are they?'

'Luke's mobile phone records.' Moore passed him the printout. 'I haven't had chance to look at them in detail yet but they confirm that he was in contact with the brothers.'

Gallagher ran his finger down the list of numbers and gave a low whistle of surprise as he halted at one of them.

'That's not the only thing that they would appear to confirm,' he said. He took his notebook out of his jacket pocket. 'That Peterborough number that Luke rang several times is very familiar.'

The sergeant flicked through several pages of notes before stopping to check something.

'Well, well, well,' he said. 'It looks like there *is* a connection between our murder and what's been happening up here, after all.'

'How so?' asked Moore, walking across to look over his shoulder. 'Whose number is it?'

'It's the landline for Carl Bradby's private investigations business and Luke rang him several times, including on the day before the murder. All fairly short calls, looks like he was leaving a message.'

'That puts a different light on things,' said Moore. 'So, how come you did not make the connection yourselves? Surely, it's the kind of thing that would turn up in your routine background checks?'

'You would have hoped so,' said Gallagher. He scowled as he recalled the way that Alison Butterfield had expressed disdain for the drudgery of routine paperwork the previous day. 'But I am afraid it is a case of a young detective not doing the basics. I'm not looking forward to telling my governor. He won't be happy.'

'I wouldn't blame him. Anyway, it looks like you'll be spending more time in Scotland, after all.'

'In which case,' said Gallagher, glancing across to the kitchen at the end of the squad room and standing up, 'might I suggest that we've got time for a cuppa?'

There was a chorus of approval from the other detectives and mugs were quickly waggled in his direction.

'You can definitely stay a bit longer.' Moore grinned.

Gallagher had just switched on the kettle when his mobile rang. When he saw it was Alison Butterfield, he sighed.

'Your young officer?' said Moore.

'I am afraid so.'

'Do you want me to go somewhere where I can't hear you disembowelling her?'

'No, it's fine,' said the sergeant, chuckling at the joke. He took the call. 'Alison, just the person.'

'Oh, dear, that sounds ominous,' said Alison Butterfield cheerfully.

'I'm afraid it is.'

'Have I done something wrong?' she asked. Anxiety had crept into her voice as she noted his serious tone of voice.

'I fear so. Did you get anywhere on those checks on Carl Bradby's business landline?'

'I asked the phone company for a list of calls,' said Butterfield.

'And have they sent it?'

'I am still waiting for it,' said the constable; now she was sounding defensive. 'Why, what's…?'

'Have you chased them up?'

'Not yet, no, I didn't think…'

'And are you still trying to track down his office so we can get our hands on the answering machine?'

'No, like I said, I was having problems finding it.'

'The machine must be somewhere, though,' said Gallagher. 'Did you not keep looking?'

Butterfield hesitated.

'Well?' said Gallagher.

'Look, if I'm honest, I haven't really been chasing it,' she admitted. 'What with all the other things that have been happening, it was kind of forgotten.'

'But I told you to keep trying. If you had done so, you would have come up with a link between Carl Bradby and the Probert brothers. As it is, I had to be told about it by the cops up here, which has not exactly been good for our reputation. It makes us look like a bunch of amateurs.'

Butterfield was silent for a few moments as she digested the information and the enormity of her error rapidly became clear.

'How much trouble am I in?' she asked in a small voice.

'Well, I don't think the DCI will be impressed,' replied Gallagher. 'You know his view on getting the basics right. Might I suggest that if you had focused on doing the job right instead of telling him how to run CID…'

Gallagher did not feel the need to complete the sentence; he felt that his message was already clear enough.

Chapter eighteen

Harris and Strothers were experiencing starkly contrasting emotions as they questioned an unshaven Graham Probert in one of the interview rooms at the police station. Harris kept glancing at the wall clock as he considered when he and Gallagher could reasonably excuse themselves and head back south, and Strothers was trying not to appear too smug as she enjoyed Graham's discomfort and the resigned body language of his sharply dressed lawyer Geoffrey Darnell.

'Might I suggest,' said Darnell, 'that there is little to be achieved by dragging proceedings out this morning? My client realises that there is no point in him denying his involvement in what happened last night. He and his brother are, as I believe is the common parlance, "bang to rights".'

'They certainly are,' said Strothers cheerfully.

'In which case, Graham is prepared to make a statement, as will Jimmy when he is well enough. I will require more time to agree our response to the suggestion that they tipped chemicals into other rivers.' Darnell looked at Strothers. 'Can I assume that Graham will be granted bail?'

'No, you can't. We'll be seeking a remand in custody.'

'I very much doubt that the court will do that,' said the solicitor. 'In my experience, the legal system accords crimes against wildlife considerably less priority than those against human beings.'

'Which is why we will also be charging Graham in connection with threats made against Gregor McAllister, who agreed to make a statement.'

'Now hang on a minute,' said Graham.

'I imagine that the court will take a dim view of a couple of thugs trying to intimidate an elderly witness in his own home, particularly a war hero who was wounded in the service of his country,' said Strothers. 'What do you think, Mr Darnell?'

The solicitor, who could not conceal his irritation at the way that he had been outmanoeuvred, did not answer her question. Instead, he tried to regain the initiative by switching his attention to Harris.

'Do I assume that your presence here indicates that you are persisting with the ridiculous suggestion that my clients murdered this Bradby fellow?' he asked.

'We're certainly investigating the possibility,' said Harris. He tried to emulate Strothers' confident demeanour but it did not come over as convincing and everyone in the room knew it.

'I am afraid that you are very much mistaken,' said Darnell. 'But you already know that, I fancy.'

'Yeah,' said Graham, regaining some of his natural belligerence. 'We ain't never heard of him so there's no way we could have killed him, is there?'

'I guess there would be a sort of logic to that suggestion were it not for the fact that you knew that he was investigating your illegal activities,' Harris said. 'That gives you a pretty strong motive to see him silenced, might I suggest?'

'Motive possibly,' said Darnell, 'but do you have anything that remotely resembles evidence?'

Harris did not reply.

'No, I thought not,' said the solicitor.

Harris scowled as Darnell made a point of deliberately turning away from the Levton Bridge detective and focusing instead on Strothers.

'I would like a minute or two with my client to discuss last night's events,' he said. 'I take it that would be acceptable?'

Strothers nodded and the detectives left the interview room and started to walk along the corridor in the direction of the stairs.

'Don't mind Geoffrey Darnell,' said Strothers. 'He's a slippery customer.'

'What hurts is that he's right,' said Harris. He glanced at his watch just as Gallagher came round the corner. 'It's time me and Matty made tracks, I think. There's nothing for us here.'

'I wouldn't be so sure about that,' said the sergeant. He held up the printouts of the phone records. 'Looks like you might be right after all, guv.'

'Sometimes, I am so good that even I do not know how I do it,' said Harris. 'Or, as on this occasion, what I have done. Right about what, Matty lad?'

'Right about employing a trusty sergeant who never lost faith in you.'

'Oh, aye,' said Harris. 'That'll be it.'

A couple of minutes later, the Levton Bridge detectives entered the interview room and sat down, to the surprise of Darnell and his client, who viewed their confident expressions with unease.

'Now then, Graham,' said Harris affably. 'About this murder you say you know nothing about…'

Chapter nineteen

'So what have we got here?' asked Maureen Strothers. She looked across the desk at Harris and Gallagher, who were sitting in her office, sipping tea from mugs. 'What's the link between Carl Bradby, the Proberts and Luke McAllister? Or are we adding up two and two and making five?'

'I think there's a link,' said Gallagher.

'There's certainly enough to keep us interested,' said Harris.

It was mid-morning and Harris and Gallagher had just emerged from their interview with Graham Probert, who, faced with the new evidence, had answered 'no comment' to every one of their questions on the instructions of Geoffrey Darnell. The solicitor's guarded performance, and the uneasy demeanour of his client, had only served to strengthen the officers' suspicions that they were hiding something.

'But what *is* the link?' asked Strothers. She took a drink of tea. 'I can see why the Proberts might want your guy Bradby dead but I'm not sure where Luke McAllister fits into the story.'

'No, neither am I,' said Harris. 'But one thing's certain; for the moment, the focus of our investigation has swung back here.'

The inspector's mobile rang; the caller was Gillian Roberts. Harris was about to put the call on speaker so they could all hear when Helen Moore walked into the office.

'Do you have a moment, ma'am?' she said.

Strothers nodded and Harris went out into the corridor to take the call from Roberts.

'Morning, Jack,' said Roberts' voice. 'Are you on your way back?'

'We would have been,' said Harris, who as was his wont, paced up and down the corridor while he was having his phone conversation. 'But it looks like there is more to this than meets the eye.'

'I thought you said there wasn't anything of interest?'

'Yeah, I did but the cops up here have turned up phone records that suggest otherwise. Turns out that there's a local lad by the name of Luke McAllister, a shady character who was drummed out of the Army in disgrace and who's been in regular contact with both Carl Bradby and the Probert brothers.'

'Intriguing,' said Roberts. 'But if it's phone records, how come we did not find that out for ourselves?'

'We probably would have done had Alison Butterfield done her job instead of spending all her time complaining about every decision I take.'

'Ah,' said Roberts. 'Do you want me to have a word with her?'

'Matty had a word on the phone. I'll talk to her about it when I get back.'

'Is it going to get heavy?' asked Roberts. 'Disciplinary?'

'I suspect it won't get that far but, hopefully, it will teach her a lesson.'

'Hopefully,' said Roberts. 'Anyway, the reason I was ringing you was to ask if you are anywhere near a television?'

'A television?' said Harris, just as a uniformed officer walked past him.

'There's one in the sergeants' room,' said the officer and turned to point back down the corridor. 'Third door on the left.'

Harris nodded his thanks.

'Yeah, I've got one, Gillian,' he said. 'Why?'

'Can I suggest that you get yourself in front of it at eleven o'clock?' said Roberts. 'The Press Office have just had a call from Sky News, saying that Sebastian de la Roche is going to hold a press conference at the estate and they want us to give them our reaction afterwards. Apparently, he has told them that it's going to be explosive stuff so they have decided to broadcast it live.'

'That's all we need,' said Harris gloomily. 'Like I told Matty, the last thing we need is investigation by media. Any idea what he is going to say?'

'I've got a pretty good idea after I went to see him last night. I reckon that he's going to have a go at us for trying to make out that he and Ronny Carroll are murderers, instead of offering him and his family protection. I suspect that he'll make it personal and single you out.'

'Yeah, I'll bet he will. He has been waiting for an opportunity like this,' said Harris. 'I'll ring you after he's done his thing.'

Harris headed back to Strothers' office.

'One thing's certain,' he said as he walked back into the room. 'The focus of our investigation has swung back to Levton Bridge.'

'Make your mind up,' said Strothers.

A few minutes later, with their mugs refilled with fresh tea, the three detectives were sitting in the sergeants' room, watching Sebastian de la Roche as he was filmed striding purposefully along the riverbank towards the waiting media. Strothers surveyed his tweed garb and deerstalker and raised an eyebrow.

'Boy, he looks the part,' she said.

'Depends what you think the part is,' said Harris. 'If you are thinking "twat", you're right.'

Strothers chuckled.

'Actually, I was thinking country gent,' she said.

'That's the image he likes to present to the world,' said Harris. 'Claims to be descended from French aristocracy.'

'Do I take it that he's not?' said Strothers.

'Actually, he's from Matty's neck of the woods. Isn't that right, Matty lad?'

'Pinner,' said the sergeant with a grin. 'His dad was called Alf Barnett and ran a tobacconists and his mother was called Elsie and worked as a dinner lady at a local school!'

Strothers laughed again.

'Don't you love people?' she said.

On the screen, Sebastian de la Roche stopped walking and stood in silence, allowing his audience to take in the scenery, the sparkling waters of the Lev dancing in the bright morning sun, the tree branches reaching down causing ripples as they gently stroked the surface.

'It's a beautiful spot,' said Strothers.

'It's where Carl Bradby's body was found,' said Harris gloomily.

'Clearly, your Mr de la Roche has a finely tuned sense of the dramatic,' said Strothers.

Harris grunted.

On the television screen, La Roche began his address to the assembled journalists, photographers and camera operators.

'Good morning, ladies and gentlemen,' he said gravely. 'As you will be aware, three days ago the body of Carl Bradby was found on this very spot by one of my members of staff. I asked the local police not to disclose the location to the media, but this was ignored with the entirely predictable result that, since then, the people that work here have been under siege by people making uninformed and scurrilous allegations, including the preposterous suggestion that I ordered one of my members of staff to kill Mr Bradby. Even worse, the police, led by Detective Chief Inspector Jack Harris, appear to agree with the rumourmongers, on the basis that Mr Bradby had been hired by the environmental pressure group Dark Waters to investigate us. The suggestion could not be further from the truth, ladies and gentlemen. I did not order anyone to murder him, nor did any of my staff carry out the act. We are as much the victims as anyone here.'

'Ha!' Harris snorted.

'Ideally, I would not go public with something like this,' said La Roche. 'However, I find myself with no alternative so that people realise that the situation is spiralling out of control.'

'At least there's something we can agree on,' murmured Harris.

'Last night,' continued La Roche, 'I received a visit from a senior officer acting on behalf of DCI Harris, who has not had the decency to get in touch with me himself. She informed me that the lunatic fringe that run the Anti-Fishing Alliance have jumped on the bandwagon and are planning some action against us as part of their deranged campaign to have fishing banned. Ladies and gentlemen, this is an appalling onslaught on the rights of anglers to enjoy their favourite pastime. You might have expected that, in the light of recent events, that my request for police protection would have met with a sympathetic response, particularly since DCI Harris is himself a keen fisherman. However, my plea for help was rejected, leaving my staff and my family even more frightened and vulnerable.'

The estate owner stared into the Sky News camera.

'DCI Harris,' he said. 'If you are listening to this, and I am sure you are, be in no doubt that if any of us are harmed as a result of your actions, the police, and you in particular, will be held directly responsible.'

And with that, he turned and walked back along the riverbank, ignoring the shouted questions from the journalists.

'He's not a fan then?' said Strothers, looking at Harris. 'I take it you are a keen fisherman?'

The inspector nodded.

'Then how come you're not offering him protection?' she said.

'Whether I am an angler or not is irrelevant,' said Harris. 'It's like the situation you found yourself in with the Proberts. You can't cover everything and I also have a superintendent who would be highly unlikely to free up the resources that we would need.'

The inspector's mobile phone rang.

'Talk of the Devil,' he said.

Strothers gave him a sympathetic look. Secretly, she was enjoying the sight of someone else having to endure superintendent troubles. Guessing what she was thinking, Harris gave a rueful smile and walked out into the corridor to take the call. He did not return for twenty-five minutes.

'That took a long time,' said Gallagher when Harris returned. 'You discussing your appointment as Head of School Crossings? Are you going to get your own lollipop stick?'

Harris gave him a mock-pained look.

'Not quite,' he said.

'So what did the great man have to say?' asked Gallagher.

'He's not exactly enamoured with the idea of, in his words, "a bunch of misguided fanatics careering round the place while engaged in internecine feuds",' replied Harris. 'He wants it stamping on before it gets out of hand and he's going to stage a press conference warning them that the valley is not the place to settle their disagreements.'

'Yeah, like they'll listen,' said Gallagher. 'And he'd better not refer to "misguided fanatics engaged in internecine feuds" when he addresses the journos, either. That will only inflame things.'

'I'm sure he won't,' said Harris. 'You know what he's like. As diplomatic as they come. He'll need to be, mind.'

'Where do you stand on the issue?' asked Strother. 'Presumably, you don't think angling should be banned?'

'I stand on the side of the decent angler,' said Harris. 'And I don't go for all this guff about fishing being cruel, either. There's plenty of scientific research to disprove it.'

'And I can't see how sticking a hook in a fish's gob can be anything other than cruel,' said Gallagher. 'And I'm a big stickleback man.'

'City boy,' said Harris, but it was a good-natured comment and he did not seem irritated.

'Do I take it that your superintendent wants you to head back?' asked Strothers. 'Because I was going to suggest that you might go with me to see Luke McAllister? We need to know what the connection is between him and Carl Bradby.'

'We certainly do,' said Harris. He downed the last of his tea and had just got to his feet when his mobile rang again. 'Bloody hell, will the thing never stop ringing?'

It was Gillian Roberts again and the inspector sat back down and placed the device on the desk with the speaker on so that the others could hear.

'I take it that Curtis got hold of you?' she said.

'Yeah, I've just come off the phone with him. Not sure I was able to offer him much information about the links up here, though.'

'Then allow me to enlighten you,' said Roberts. They could sense from her voice that she was pleased with herself. 'After you told me about Luke McAllister, I rang my friendly Army guy and asked if he had ever heard of him. It turns out that in the final months before he left the Army, Carl Bradby was seconded to the Military Police and guess who ended up in one of the cells he was looking after?'

'Not a certain Luke McAllister, by any chance?' said Harris.

'The very same,' said Roberts. 'It turns out that the last offence for which he was locked up occurred when he was at Hereford on a training course. A fight with a couple of locals, apparently. I am wondering if Luke held a grudge against Bradby from those days. I mean, MPs are not exactly the most popular characters, are they?'

'They certainly aren't,' said Harris. 'Well, there's only one way to find out.'

He ended the call and headed for the door.

'Can I make a suggestion?' said Strothers as she and Gallagher followed Harris into the corridor. 'Three of us to interview Luke may be a bit much so, Jack, maybe you and me can see him, and Matty, you can join our team searching the Proberts' industrial unit? Who knows, it may turn up something of use for your investigation?'

'Makes sense,' said Gallagher.

'Let's do that then,' said Harris.

With events threatening to spiral out of control, it felt good to be making decisions again.

Chapter twenty

Jack Harris's sense that he was back in control lasted until he and Strothers arrived at the village of Lane End in the inspector's Land Rover to be confronted by the sight of an ambulance and a police patrol vehicle parked outside Gregor McAllister's cottage.

'The older feller, you reckon?' said Strothers.

'It's very suspicious, if it is,' said Harris, parking nearby and cutting the engine. 'An hour and a half after he tells you that he will make a statement against the Proberts and here he is, being carted off to hospital? Being involved with Carl Bradby is a dangerous occupation.'

As the grim-faced detectives pushed their way through the front gate and started to walk up the path, a couple of paramedics emerged from the cottage, carrying a stretcher which bore the unconscious figure of Gregor McAllister. Strothers flashed her warrant card and the paramedics stopped walking so that the detectives could take a look at the old man. It was not an encouraging sight; his eyes were closed, his skin was grey and his breathing was shallow, but the most alarming feature was the deep gash in his forehead, from which blood seeped, soaking through the bandaging. Harris frowned, reminded of the type of injury that Carl Bradby had sustained.

'An accident?' Strothers asked the paramedics. 'A fall?'

'I wouldn't have said so,' replied one of them. 'It looks more like an assault to me.'

'How bad is he?' asked Harris.

'Too early to say. He'd not been lying there long before his grandson found him and rung it in. If the lad had arrived home much later, there's a good chance that his grandfather would have been beyond saving.'

'That's lucky,' said Strothers.

'Depends who hit him,' said the paramedic pointedly.

'What do you mean?' asked Strothers. 'Do you think the grandson might have done it?'

'Ask your guys. They'll tell you. They're in the house with him.'

The detectives were met at the front door by a uniformed constable.

'You got here quickly,' he said in surprise. 'I've only just come off the phone from CID.'

'We were on our way here anyway,' said Strothers. 'The paramedic said that it was Luke who found him. Is that right?'

'Yeah, it is. He's in the living room.' The constable went over to close the door so that their conversation could not be overheard.

'The paramedic said that you might think it's an iffy one?' Strothers said.

'I reckon so,' said the constable. 'How come you were on your way here, ma'am? Was it to see Luke?'

'Yeah, he's fallen in with the wrong crowd,' said Strothers. 'Why do you think it's iffy?'

'When we asked him what happened, he took a funny turn, and said that he needed to sit down. And there's no sign of a break-in or anyone forcing their way into the house so it's highly likely that he was attacked by someone he knows.'

'Any sign of a weapon?' asked Harris.

'Not that we can find,' said the constable.

Strothers led the way into the living room, where Luke was sitting in an armchair with his eyes closed. He opened them when they arrived.

'How's Grandad?' he asked in a voice that trembled slightly.

'I'm not sure,' said Strothers. 'What happened? Where did you find him?'

Luke pointed to a bloodstained rug in the corner of the room.

'He was lying over there,' he said. He shuddered at the memory. 'I thought he was dead at first. It was horrible.'

'What time was this?' asked Strothers.

'Just after ten,' he said. 'I spent last night at my girlfriend's place and had just got back.'

'You couldn't have missed his attacker by much then. I talked to him on the phone just after nine and he was OK then.'

'You talked to him?' The revelation seemed to have unsettled Luke. 'What about?'

'He agreed to give us a statement about the way the Proberts tried to intimidate him,' said Strothers. 'You know what your grandfather's like, always keen to do the right thing.'

'Do you think it was the Proberts that attacked him then?'

'No. We arrested them last night and they are still in custody,' said Strothers.

'Arrested for what?' asked Luke.

'Dumping chemicals,' said Strothers. She gave Luke a hard look. 'Can we drop the charade, please? I reckon that you know all this already. I think that your grandfather told you.'

'How could he?' protested Luke. 'I told you, he was unconscious when I found him. He didn't say anything.'

'But I think he did,' said Strothers. 'I think that's why he's on his way to hospital.'

Luke's anxiety had been replaced by something more guarded.

'Surely, you don't think that I attacked him?' he said. 'My own grandfather? I would never do anything like that. I love him.'

'Maybe you do,' said Strothers. 'But my guess is that you wanted to protect the Proberts and stop him giving his statement.'

'Why would I try to protect them?' exclaimed Luke. Beads of sweat had begun to appear on his forehead. 'I've got no time for people like them. You know that.'

'Then why do you have Graham's number on your mobile phone?' asked Harris, speaking for the first time. 'And why are you in regular contact with him?'

Luke gave the inspector a suspicious look.

'How do you know that?' he asked.

'The same way we know that you were in contact with Carl Bradby on a number of occasions before he was murdered,' said Harris. He gave Strothers a nod. 'You have some questions to answer, young man.'

Strothers produced a set of handcuffs.

'Luke McAllister,' she said. 'You are under arrest on suspicion of the attempted murder of your grandfather.'

The blood drained from Luke's face and he closed his eyes and allowed himself to be led from the room without further protest.

Chapter twenty-one

Luke McAllister still appeared to be overwhelmed by shock an hour later as he walked into the police station interview room in the company of his solicitor. Harris and Strothers knew that their suspect had seen a lawyer but did not know the man's identity until he followed his client through the door. The officers failed to hide their surprise.

'Mr Darnell,' said Strothers as the solicitor sat down at the table. 'Who on earth would have thought it?'

'I take it that you do not have a problem with my attending the interview?' asked Darnell. 'It is, after all, a free world.'

'Not at your rates, it isn't,' said Strothers.

Darnell gave a thin smile, opened his briefcase, produced a notepad, and took a pen from his jacket pocket, which he placed rather deliberately next to the pad, taking care to make sure that it was straight.

'I must admit to being rather surprised to see you here,' said Strothers. 'If your client was hoping to put some distance between himself and the Proberts, this is hardly the way to do it. The fact that they have the same solicitor only serves to strengthen our suspicion that Luke attacked his grandfather to protect them.'

'Have you heard how Grandad is?' asked Luke anxiously. Mention of the old man seemed to bring him out of his state of shock.

'He's being assessed by the doctors,' said Strothers. 'We'll know more later this morning but the signs are not good.'

'For the record, my client denies being responsible for the assault,' said Darnell.

'Nevertheless, he does admit to being at the cottage on or around the time when Gregor was attacked,' said Strothers.

'I hardly think "admitted" is the word, Chief Inspector. It is his home, after all. Where else would you expect him to go?' The solicitor turned his attention to Harris. 'I assume that you are here because it's something to do with your ill-advised efforts to establish a connection between the Proberts and the death of Carl Bradby?'

'Indeed,' said Harris.

'Well, I can't help feeling that you are wasting your time – and mine, for that matter,' said Darnell. He gave a slight smile. 'However, as your colleague so adroitly pointed out, my hourly rate is far in excess of yours so I have no objection to playing along for a while. Which of you wants to go first?'

Harris glanced at Strothers. Never one with a reputation for handling the politics that came with the job, he was determined not to jeopardise the good working relationship that he had developed with the Police Scotland officer, for whom he had already developed a deep respect. Appreciating the gesture, Strothers nodded her approval.

'So, Luke,' said Harris, 'as your solicitor observed, I suspect that your relationship with the Proberts may have something to do with the assault on Carl Bradby, so let's start there. Why do you talk regularly to Graham on his mobile?'

Luke glanced at his lawyer for guidance. Darnell shook his head.

'No comment,' said Luke.

'My client will give the same answer to each of your questions,' said the solicitor.

'I am afraid that "no comment" is not good enough,' said Harris. He was trying to ignore the headache that had started to come on as lack of sleep started to catch up with him, and was in no mood for the solicitor's games. 'Your client really needs to tell us what happened. Might I remind both of you that, if Gregor dies, this will become a murder inquiry?'

'I hardly think we need reminding of that,' said Darnell tartly. 'However, if my client does not wish to answer your questions then there is nothing I can do.'

Sensing that if he was not careful, he would lose the initiative again, Harris decided to gamble on a theory which he had been crystallising in his mind for some time.

'Come on, Luke,' he said. 'We all know that Graham Probert rings you for help when he's dumping the chemicals.'

Harris glanced at Strothers.

'Isn't that right, Chief Inspector?' he said.

'It certainly is,' replied Strothers. She tried to conceal her surprise at the new approach; it was not something they had discussed.

'Who told you that I helped them dump chemicals?' asked Luke, looking increasingly anxious. 'Was it Graham?'

'It certainly was not,' said Darnell quickly. 'Don't listen to them. It's a trick, and a cheap one at that and I would strongly advise–'

'What would your grandfather think if he found out what you have been doing?' asked Harris, ignoring the lawyer's protestations. 'I imagine that he would be horrified to think that you were one of the people who destroyed his beloved river. Or does he know already,

Luke? Is that what this morning was about? Did you argue about it?'

'What happened this morning was an accident,' said Luke, his voice trembling with emotion as his resolved crumbled. 'I didn't mean to hurt him and I was never the one who put the stuff in the rivers, neither. It was the Proberts. I told Grandad that.'

Darnell opened his mouth to raise an objection but Luke did not give him the chance.

'I want to tell them!' he said vehemently. 'I'm sick of living a lie! I'm not proud of what I have done and the worst thing is that I have let my grandfather down far too many times. I want to do the right thing, for once. I owe him that.'

'Tell us what happened then,' said Harris. 'From the beginning.'

Darnell was about to try his protest again but thought better of it when Harris gave him a fierce look. Jack Harris was back in control and the solicitor knew when he was beaten. He shrugged and stayed silent. The detectives allowed the time Luke needed to compose his thoughts.

'Can you imagine what it's like having a war hero for a grandfather?' Luke said eventually. 'I'm not trying to use it as an excuse but someone like me has no chance of ever living up to those standards. I wanted to show Grandad that I was at least making an effort, to give him a reason to be proud of me like I am proud of him, but I was turned down for every job that I went for. The moment they read my Army record, that was it.'

'I can understand that,' said Harris. 'But you're right, it's no excuse.'

'I know, but it might help to explain what happened. I met the Proberts when I was drinking in a Glasgow pub with some pals one night and we got talking. We got on really well and Graham rang me two days later and asked me to go and see him.'

'Why?' asked Harris.

'He said that I was someone he could trust and would I like to work for him?'

'Doing what?' asked Strothers.

'Well, that's the thing,' said Luke. 'It was nothing heavy, selling stolen stuff on, mainly. Although the brothers didn't pay much, at least they paid something so I told Grandad that I'd got a job in a shop two days a week and offered to start putting a bit towards the upkeep of the house, food, that sort of thing. I could see that he was proud of the effort I was making and that meant everything to me.'

'I am assuming that working for the Proberts did not stop at handling stolen goods?' said Harris.

'After a couple of months, Graham said that they'd started disposing of chemicals but that the costs were too high so they had decided to start dumping the stuff illegally instead and he wanted me to help them.'

Geoffrey Darnell closed his eyes and tried to imagine that he was somewhere else.

'Why you?' asked Strothers.

'Graham said that they knew nothing about rivers but thought I might. I'd mentioned that I like going fishing and he wanted me to find places that they could use.'

'And you said yes?' said Harris. He shook his head in disbelief. 'Even though you knew the damage that it would cause?'

'I refused at first,' said Luke, a defensive tone to his voice. 'I told them what it would do to Grandad if he found out that I was involved in something like that. Graham said that he didn't care and that if I said no, he would tell him that the job in the shop did not exist. I couldn't disappoint Grandad again. Besides, Graham said that he'd pay me £500 each time we got rid of a load of chemicals. I explained the extra money by telling Grandad that I'd been promoted to assistant manager in the shop. He was really chuffed.'

'But surely, you realised the damage you would be causing?'

'Of course, I did, but the first couple of times we did it, the chemicals did not seem to do much. The lads assured me that they were fairly weak so I didn't think there was anything to worry about. I'm not sure anyone even knew what we had done.'

'But that changed when you chose the Caine?'

Luke nodded. He was fighting strong emotions now and the words were tumbling out.

'The chemicals must have been stronger. I don't think Graham and Jimmy ever really checked what they were handling. They just took the money.' He paused with tears glistening in his eyes. 'You know the rest. It was a disaster.'

'It certainly was,' said Harris.

'I tried to get out of it after that – I couldn't bear seeing Grandad so upset – but Graham said that I was in too deep and that he'd hate for anything to happen to my grandfather. I think that's why they went to see him that night. It wasn't so much a message for him but for me.'

'So what happened this morning?' asked Strothers.

The tears started to run down Luke's cheeks and it took him the best part of a minute to compose himself enough to be able to relive the event. Eventually, he looked at Strothers.

'Grandad had just come off the phone to you when I got there,' he said in a voice that was so quiet that the detectives had to lean forward in order to hear him. 'He told me that he had agreed to give you a statement about the intimidation. I told him that if the brothers were arrested for it, things would go badly for me, that I would probably go to prison. Grandad was horrified – he'd had no idea what I had been doing – and he started shouting at me. The window was open and I was afraid that someone might hear – a lot of people use the path, dog walkers, joggers – but he wouldn't shut up. He said he didn't care who heard then he stepped forward with his hand raised and I lashed out at him. It was instinct. I didn't mean to do it. He fell over and hit his head on the floor.'

Luke fell silent for a few moments.

'What happens if he dies?' he asked eventually.

'If what you say is true, then you may well be looking at a charge of manslaughter,' said Strothers. 'It would help if you agreed to a make a statement saying what the Proberts have been doing. Are you prepared to do that?'

Luke nodded.

'If Grandad was prepared to do it, then so will I,' he said.

Geoffrey Darnell gave a quiet sigh; it was clear to the solicitor that his efforts to protect the Probert brothers were consigned to abject failure and he was already dreading his next encounter with them.

'Tell me about Carl Bradby,' said Harris. 'Where does he fit into things?'

'I didn't kill him, if that's what you are thinking.'

'But you did know him, didn't you? You met him when you were in the Army, I think?'

'That gives it an air of respectability that I don't deserve,' said Luke with a hollow laugh. 'He was a military policeman and locked me up when I was based in Hereford. We got talking one day and got on really well. He said that he'd try to help me when I left the Army. He said he was looking to start his own investigations agency and said there might be some work to come out of it.'

'And did you get any work from him?' asked Harris.

'No. I rang the number on the card he gave me and left a message and he rang me back a few times – that's the way we communicated, he never gave me his mobile number – but nothing came of it. He said there was barely enough work for one.'

'Why did you ring him not long before he was killed?'

'I left a message on his machine to warn him that the Proberts had found out about his investigation into the chemical dumping and that Jimmy had suggested that they kill him.'

'And how do you know that Jimmy had said that?' asked Harris.

'Because I was there when he said it. We were having a glass of whisky in the workshop one night.'

'Was it you that gave them Carl's name?'

'No, I wouldn't do that. Carl was a decent bloke. No, Graham said that they had received an anonymous call telling them who he was.'

'Do you know if Jimmy followed through on his threat?' asked Harris. 'Did he kill Carl Bradby?'

'I doubt it. Graham told me later that he'd managed to persuade him to drop the idea. Mind, you never know with Jimmy.'

'Weren't you taking a huge risk warning Carl?' asked Strothers. 'Wasn't there a danger that the Proberts would find out what you'd done?'

'Yes, but I wanted to make amends. I felt I owed it to Grandad.'

'Did Carl ring you back after you warned him?' asked Harris.

'Yeah. He said that I should not worry, that he could handle himself.' Luke frowned. 'Clearly, he was wrong. He couldn't handle himself.'

'That,' said Harris, standing up, 'may be the understatement of the year.'

'I take it there's no way that this can be kept from the Proberts?' asked Luke.

'I very much doubt it,' said Harris. 'Even if we did not tell them, I suspect your solicitor would.'

Darnell nodded.

'Well, at least everything is out in the open,' said Luke. 'That's something. There was one more thing. Something Carl said. I don't know if it's relevant but you might want to know…'

Chapter twenty-two

Harris had just parked the Land Rover in the hospital car park and was waiting for Strothers to arrive so that they could interview Jimmy Probert together, when his mobile rang.

'Gillian,' he said. 'How goes the day?'

'It was going fine until Curtis held his press conference,' said Roberts. 'He's caused all sorts of trouble.'

'Why, what's he said?'

'He'd just given the journalists some information about the Anti-Fishing Alliance and tried to move on to something else but they kept banging on about you. Where were you? Why weren't you briefing them? Were you still running the inquiry? Had you been moved on to other things because as a keen angler you're too close to it? That sort of thing.'

'It's nice to be missed,' said Harris. 'I didn't know they cared.'

'Yeah, well, it got to Curtis big time and he said that the last thing he needed was the media stirring up trouble when we already had… hang on, let me find the exact words…' There was a pause and Harris could hear the detective inspector flicking through her notebook.

'Not "misguided fanatics engaged in internecine feuds" by any chance?' said Harris.

'Yeah, that's the phrase he used. How do you know that?'

'He mentioned it when I talked to him.'

'Well, anyway, social media has gone crazy, calls for him to be sacked, all that sort of thing. I've put a call into Leckie to see if Miriam Coles posts anything in response on their website. I fear the worst, Jack, I really do. This could easily spiral out of control. When will you be back in Levton Bridge? We could really do with you.'

'Yeah, I know. I've got a couple of things to tidy up here then I'll be on my way. Oh, by the way, we've just picked up an interesting snippet. We've just come from interviewing Luke McAllister and he reckons that there's a woman involved somehow.'

'A woman?'

'Yeah, according to Luke, he was talking to Carl a few days ago when he mentioned that he had a girlfriend,' said Harris. 'When he tried to find out more about her, Carl clammed up.'

'So we've no idea who she is?'

'I am afraid not. I'll ask Matty to have a look. Who are you sending up to work with him?'

'Alistair Marshall,' said Roberts. 'He left an hour ago.'

As the inspector was ending the call, he spotted Strothers' car pulling in and within a couple of minutes they were making their way to one of the wards on the hospital's fifth floor, where they nodded a greeting to the uniformed officer standing guard outside one of the side rooms. Jimmy Probert was sitting up in bed with his arm in a sling. He glowered at the detectives.

'What do you fuckers want?' he said.

'Oh, come now, what have we done to deserve that?' said Strothers, pretending to be offended. 'Well apart from shooting you, that is? We've been worried about you, haven't we, Jack?'

'I couldn't sleep for thinking about him,' said Harris.

Harris had moved over to the window, having noticed the faint outlines of hills in the distance. Manoeuvring himself to get a better view over the roofs of the houses surrounding the hospital, he felt a pang of regret that he was not walking in his beloved North Pennines with Scoot and Archie on such a bright late summer's day. With an effort, he turned his attention back to Jimmy Probert.

'How is the arm, anyway?' he asked.

'Like you care,' said Jimmy.

'No, you're right, I don't,' said Harris. 'Anyway, we wanted to ask if you—'

'Mr Darnell told me not to say anything to you,' said Jimmy. 'Not until he arrives anyway. Where is he?'

'I'm not sure,' said Harris. 'Is he supposed to be here?'

He glanced at Strothers, who shrugged; the detectives had deliberately arrived early for their meeting with Jimmy, gambling on the hope that Jimmy would let something slip before Geoffrey Darnell turned up and things became formal.

'Well, it's pointless asking me any questions,' said Jimmy. He moved his arm and gave an exaggerated look of pain. 'I shouldn't even be talking to you. In case you hadn't noticed, one of your trigger-happy cowboys shot me last night and the doctors say that I need rest.'

'They also say that you are fit enough to talk to us just so long as you don't get stressed,' said Strothers. 'You're not stressed are you, Jimmy?'

Jimmy gave her a baleful look.

'Besides,' said Strothers, 'we aren't going to ask you any questions. Are we, Jack?'

Jimmy looked at her suspiciously.

'You aren't?' he said.

'That's right.' Strothers sat down on the edge of the bed. 'No, we just wanted to tell you that you and Graham are being charged in connection with dumping chemicals and attempting to intimidate Gregor McAllister. You'll find out soon enough from your lawyer, so I'll tell you. Gregor was attacked at his home this morning.'

'Yeah, well, you can't pin that on me!' said Jimmy. 'I was here!'

'Yes, we know that,' said Strothers. She gave a slight smile. 'We're not that stupid, Jimmy. And don't get some cockamamie idea into your head and go looking for the old man, because he's not in this hospital.'

'Who attacked him?' asked Jimmy.

'Your pal Luke. You know him pretty well, I think? He certainly knows you. Mr Darnell told him not to say anything to us as well but, oddly enough, once we got him talking, we just couldn't shut him up, could we, Jack?'

Harris looked away from the window.

'That's right, and very interesting it proved to be, too,' he said. 'Who would have thought that they dumped chemicals in so many rivers?'

'Who would think it indeed?' said Strothers.

Jimmy looked increasingly anxious and Harris gave a thin smile; it was time to drop the final bombshell.

'Then there's the murder to consider, of course,' said Harris. He moved away from the window and over the bed where he looked down at Jimmy Probert. 'Luke seemed to be suggesting that you threatened to kill–'

'That will do!' said an angry voice.

The detectives turned to see Geoffrey Darnell enter the room.

'This is disgraceful conduct,' said the solicitor. 'I made it clear that Jimmy was not to interviewed until I was present.'

'It must have slipped my mind,' said Harris, adopting his best innocent tone of voice.

'Like hell it did.' The solicitor jabbed an accusatory finger at Harris. 'You're pushing it, Chief Inspector. I don't know how they do things where you come from, but this is way out of order and I would appreciate it if you left.'

The lawyer gave Strothers a hard look.

'I'm disappointed in you, Maureen,' he said. 'You really should know better and I'd like you to leave as well.'

'Before I go,' said Strothers. 'I'll need Jimmy to give us a statement about what happened on the riverbank last night.'

'It will have to wait,' said Darnell curtly. 'My client is very tired.'

'It can't wait for long,' said Strothers. 'There's no way he's wriggling out of this one just because he took a bullet in the arm.'

There was silence for a few moments and, when it became clear that the lawyer was not going to change his mind, the detectives left the room. They nodded to the uniformed officer on guard again and walked through the ward in the direction of the stairs.

'You really are all heart, aren't you?' said Harris. 'And that poor man lying in his hospital bed.'

'Well, what do you expect me to say?' said Strothers. 'I know that weasel of a lawyer of old and you can bet your bottom dollar that he is working on a way of using Jimmy's injury to his advantage. Talking of weasel tricks, I meant to mention it earlier, but the next time you pull a stroke like telling Luke that you knew he was helping the Proberts dump chemicals, let me know in advance, will you? I nearly fell off my chair.'

'I wondered when you'd mention it,' said Harris, with a slight smile. 'It worked, didn't it?'

Strothers nodded.

'It did,' she said. 'What's your thinking on Jimmy? Do you think he followed through on his threat and murdered Carl Bradby?'

'Not really,' said Harris as they reached the top of the stairs. 'He's a hothead who acts before he thinks but it's all circumstantial. We'll just have to hope that the search of their offices turns something up, not that I'm particularly hopeful.'

* * *

One look at Matty Gallagher as he stood outside Kwikkie Waste Disposal suggested that Harris was right not to be hopeful. The brothers' business occupied a single-storey building on a rundown industrial estate on the edge of Glasgow, all grimy windows and weeds poking through cracked tarmac, and the sergeant was standing with hands thrust into his anorak pockets as he watched forensics personnel in white overalls lifting up piles of sacking and conducting searches of company vehicles. Harris parked the Land Rover and, while Strothers went to find Helen Moore, the inspector walked over to Gallagher.

'Matty lad,' he said. 'Do I take it that things are not going well?'

'They are if you've got the Police Scotland logo on your jacket,' said Gallagher. 'There's tonnes of stuff linking the brothers with the chemicals. However, there's nothing to connect the brothers to our murder.'

'I'm not surprised. If there is anything, it's going to come from interviewing the brothers again. Alistair's on his way up so it might be worth having another talk to Graham when he gets here. Jimmy didn't give us anything. However, there's a new angle worth chasing up. According to Luke, Carl Bradby had a girlfriend.'

'Do we know who she is?'

'No, but I would very much like to find out.'

'I take it you're heading back?'

'Yeah, I think so.' The inspector's mobile phone rang and he took the call. 'Mr Leckie, as I live and breathe, how goes it?'

'The next time your commander slags you off for your lack of diplomatic skills, can I suggest that you remind him about this morning?' said Leckie.

'I heard that he lost it in the press conference.'

'And very entertaining it would have been were the situation not so serious. He's irritated the fragrant Ms Coles big time. Oddly enough, she's notoriously touchy when people call her a deranged lunatic. I've sent you a link. Same set-up as last time. Click on the fish and key in the code. It's *5218* this time. Ring me back when you've seen her video, will you? I sense a joint operation coming on.'

Harris and Gallagher went to sit in the Land Rover, where the inspector clicked through on the link as instructed and Miriam Coles appeared on the screen, not standing on a riverbank this time but sitting at a table in a non-descript office. She looked angry.

'Good morning,' she said through pursed lips. 'Since my last message, we have seen the Anti-Fishing Alliance subjected to a tirade of abuse from people who should know better. That sleazeball Sebastian de la Roche gave a press conference in which he described us as "deranged" and "lunatics" and claimed that we are depriving anglers of the rights to fish, without acknowledging the right of the fish to live free of pain. Then the local police commander, a stuffed shirt called Philip Curtis, told the media that we are "misguided fanatics careering round the place while engaged in internecine feuds".'

Coles gave the camera a stern look before continuing.

'I am sure that I do not need to remind you that we will not tolerate such abuse,' she said eventually. 'We never have and we never will. I would also remind you that we prefer direct action to words, which is why our executive committee has agreed to carry out an operation in the area in memory of Carl Bradby, who sacrificed his life while attempting to uncover the sordid truth about the angling community. Usual arrangement; text me if you want to be involved.'

Harris rang Leckie.

'Clearly, they plan to portray Carl Bradby as some kind of martyr,' said the inspector. 'Do we have their text details?'

'No, we have to rely on our anonymous informant but whoever it is, they tend to be pretty reliable.'

'Any idea what the plan might be, Graham?' asked Gallagher.

'It's got to be targeted at Sebastian de la Roche,' said Leckie. 'They may be wild but I can't see them targeting a police officer. What do you think, Hawk?'

'I think,' said Harris, 'that it's high time I went home.'

* * *

Within half an hour, the inspector and his dogs were heading south but had only been on the road for ten minutes when his mobile rang again. It was Stuart Liversedge.

'Now, I wonder what he wants. As if I didn't know,' murmured Harris. He took the call. 'Stuart, what can I do for you?'

'I hear you've been creating mayhem in Scotland,' said the co-founder of Dark Waters. 'Arresting the Proberts and Luke McAllister and I also heard that Jimmy got himself shot.'

'And how would you know that?' asked Harris. 'We've not put out any press releases.'

'You hear things in my line of work. Anonymous tip-offs, usually. I take it that the rumours are true?'

'They are, and you'd be well advised to remember today the next time you decide to slag the police off for sitting on our hands.'

'Touché – and well done.'

'Most of it was down to Maureen Strothers. She even has enough to make a charge stick in relation to the River Caine. You underestimated her, Stuart, she just needed time. Might I suggest that you let her have the evidence that Carl collected? I'm sure it would help.'

'I'll think about it,' said Stuart. 'Are you still in Glasgow then?'

'I'm just heading back to Levton Bridge.'

'Any chance you can drop in on me on your way back?'

'I'd rather not. It's a big detour.'

'I appreciate that, but I wouldn't ask if it wasn't important.'

'And you can't tell me on the phone?'

'I'd rather not,' said Stuart; he sounded worried. 'But things are happening that you need to know about.'

'Yeah, alright,' said Harris. 'I'll be with you in an hour or so.'

Chapter twenty-three

The headquarters of Dark Waters was still and silent when Jack Harris brought the Land Rover to a halt outside the front gate. The light was fading rapidly and, after taking a torch from the vehicle, the inspector walked along the path leading to the house. As had happened on his previous visit, he was nearing the house when the front door swung open, this time to reveal Stuart standing on his own, watching the detective's approach in solemn silence.

'Thank you for coming,' he said. 'I really do appreciate it.'

'That's alright,' said Harris. He stepped into the hallway and nodded at the suitcase on the floor as Anna emerged from the living room. She looked even more emotional than on his previous visit. 'Are you going somewhere nice?'

'I'm going to stay with my sister for a few days,' she said. 'It's a little village on the Northumberland coast. Craster.'

'I know it well. Very good for birdwatching. It's an excellent area for seabirds. In fact, if you are interested, there's a really good colony of–'

'I don't think I'll be doing much birdwatching,' said Anna. 'I'll make you a pot of tea before I go.'

'What, you're travelling now?' said Harris in surprise. 'Isn't it a bit late to set off? It's already dark.'

'I have to get away,' said Anna.

'Why, what's…?'

'Stuart can tell you what's happened,' said Anna.

She lost her fight against tears and disappeared into the kitchen. Harris gave her husband a quizzical look.

'She says that she can't stay here,' said Stuart. 'She's going to stay with her sister until this all blows over. Her nerves are in tatters.'

'What on earth's been happening? Do I take it that you've had more intimidation. Is that why you wanted to see me?'

Stuart Liversedge picked up a torch from a side table and walked towards the front door.

'Let me show you something,' he said.

He led the way between the aviaries until he stopped at the final cage, where he focused the torch's beam on a couple of holes in the timber birdhouse. Harris looked closer, then looked at Stuart.

'Are they bullet holes?' he asked.

'They are. Well, from a shotgun, to be precise.'

'What happened?'

'It was about this time yesterday,' said Stuart. 'I was settling the birds down for the night when someone fired three shots. Two of them hit the birdhouse, not far from where I was standing, and the third one missed.'

'Did you see who did it?' asked Harris.

'No, it was getting dark but I heard someone running away. Thank God Anna was not here when it happened. She was on her way back from visiting a friend and did not get back until later. She was horrified when she found out and was all for leaving then. I managed to calm her down.'

'So what changed her mind?'

'You, I suspect.'

'What have I done?' asked the inspector.

'When I told her that you were going to drop in on us, she said she couldn't bear talking about it anymore and came down the stairs with her suitcase. You can't blame her really. She's absolutely terrified.'

'I'm not surprised,' said Harris. 'Who do you think fired the shots? The Proberts?'

'Are you still looking at them for Carl's murder?'

'I don't think so, no.'

'Well, I'm having second thoughts about them as well,' said Stuart.

'Now he tells me,' said Harris. 'Why are you having second thoughts?'

'Let's go back into the house. I can tell you better over a cuppa.'

They returned to the living room just as Anna walked in carrying a tray with tea and biscuits, which she placed on a table.

'Thank you,' said Harris.

Anna nodded in acknowledgment and looked at her husband.

'I'll be off to Kathy's,' she said, then glanced at Harris. 'It's nothing personal, Chief Inspector.'

'I'd rather you stayed,' said the detective. 'I'd quite like to hear your take on what's been happening.'

'No, I can't, it's too…'

'I know you don't like talking about it, but I'll make it as quick as I can,' said Harris. 'I was just telling Stuart that we don't think the Proberts killed Carl Bradby.'

'But I thought they were your main suspects?' said Anna.

'We did consider them at one point, but not now,' said Harris. 'And I don't think that they were responsible for firing at Stuart, either. They would appear to have been in Glasgow at the time it happened. You've been having second thoughts about the Proberts as well, Stuart? Why? You seemed so sure.'

'I think that my intense loathing of them meant that I jumped to conclusions without much in the way of evidence,' said Stuart. 'I'm sorry if I misled you, Chief Inspector. I genuinely believed what I said.'

'It's understandable,' said Harris. He took a sip of tea and reached for a biscuit. 'They did have a pretty strong motive. So, who do you think we should be looking at for the murder now?'

'The other people with a strong motive,' said Stuart. 'The more I thought about it, the more I kept coming back to Ronny Carroll. Acting under orders from Sebastian de la Roche.'

'What makes you say that?' asked Harris.

'Because the more I watched La Roche ranting on about us at his press conference on the television, the more I realised that I had not appreciated the true strength of his feeling and the more likely it became that he ordered Carl's murder, as well as the attempts to frighten us into dropping the investigation. From what I hear of Ronny Carroll, he'll do whatever La Roche tells him to.'

'That's true enough,' said Harris. 'And there's a definite logic to what you say. What about you, Anna? Do you agree with Stuart?'

'I don't want to think about it,' she said unhappily.

'Well, there's certainly plenty of folk at Levton Bridge Police Station who would agree with him,' said the inspector.

'Yes, and they're not the only ones,' said Stuart. 'I hear that the Anti-Fishing Alliance are going to do something at the Langdon Estate. I don't know the details but, apparently, Miriam sees it as an opportunity to breathe new life into her group. She's jealous of our success, Chief Inspector. Do you know how many people watched the last film we posted on our website? The one showing the farmer in Shropshire felling the trees on the riverbank? Thirteen thousand, that's how many. And do you know how many hits the Anti-Fishing Alliance's website got last week?'

'No, but something tells me that you're–'

'Twenty-six,' said Stuart. 'Twenty-six! And most of them were their own members, three of whom have left the group in the past week because they don't want to be associated with Guy Robertson.'

'Why not?'

'Because he's too extreme, even for them. He's a violent man with a fearsome temper, is Guy, and the word is that his mood has become more erratic with the drugs he takes. He's out of control, Jack, and for all I detest La Roche and his loathsome water bailiff, the last thing I want is for there to be another murder when I could have done something to prevent it. That's why I asked to see you.'

'I'll see what I can do,' said Harris. He stood up and made to leave. 'One last thing, it seems that Carl Bradby may have had a girlfriend. Do either of you know anything about that?'

'It's the first I've heard of it,' said Stuart. He gave a slight smile. 'Mind you, it was not exactly the kind of thing you talked about with Carl. He did not exactly come over as the most romantic of men.'

'No, I don't suppose he did,' said Harris. 'What about you, Anna? Have you heard anything?'

The inspector asked more in hope than expectation because, throughout the conversation, her body language as she sat hunched up on the couch conveyed the clear message that she did not want to be there. Sure enough, she shook her head.

'I'm sorry but I don't know anything about that,' she said. 'Is it important?'

'Probably not,' said Harris. 'Anyway, I must make tracks. I hope the visit to your sister does you good, Anna. Drive carefully.'

She nodded but remained seated as her husband followed Harris down the hallway.

'Thank you for coming by,' said Stuart. 'It really is much appreciated.'

'No problem, and thank you for the tip-off about the AFA.'

'I thought you ought to know,' said Stuart. He opened the front door. 'And you be careful, too, yes? These are dangerous times.'

'They certainly are,' said Harris and stepped out into the night.

Stuart Liversedge's cautionary words echoed around the detective's mind as he left the house and walked along the path between the silent aviaries. Feeling the unaccustomed rush of nerves, the inspector tried to remain calm but was unable to resist the temptation to shoot uneasy looks around him as he approached the front gate and sought the telltale movement that would reveal the presence of the gunman in the gathering shadows.

It was with a sense of relief that he reached the Land Rover without incident. He sat for a few moments, looking out for Anna's car but it did not appear, so he set off on the final leg of his journey along the narrow, twisting road that would cut through the hills and take him home.

Chapter twenty-four

Things were happening, and happening fast, by the time Harris arrived back in Levton Bridge, took Scoot and Archie for a walk around the nearby park and headed for the police station. He walked into his office to find a small pile of Post-it notes on his desk from people wanting to talk to him. Having given the dogs their tea, he flicked through the messages and walked out into the corridor, leaving the animals in their customary position beneath the radiator. He was halfway down the corridor when his mobile rang. It was Gallagher.

'How's it going?' asked Harris.

'I'm not sure there's much more we can do up here,' said the sergeant. 'We've just interviewed Graham Probert again but he was doing his usual "no comment" routine, probably because he genuinely has nothing to say. I have heard nothing to think that he and Jimmy had anything do with Carl's death. Alistair agrees.'

'And so do I,' said Harris. 'And Stuart Liversedge has gone off the idea as well. He fancies La Roche and Carroll now. I take it that the Proberts have been charged with the other stuff anyway?'

'They sure have. Police Scotland have thrown the book at them. Maureen Strothers is walking round like a tom with two dicks. Gregor McAllister has regained consciousness and told her that he does not think Luke meant to hurt him. Says that he caught his foot on the rug. Maureen's got so many other things on the go, she's letting it lie. He'll be prosecuted for assisting with the chemical dumping, anyway.'

'Good,' said Harris. 'He shouldn't get away with that. Nobody should. You getting anywhere on an ID for Bradby's girlfriend?'

'No one knows anything about her,' said Gallagher. 'So, we are looking at Sebastian de la Roche and Ronny Carroll for the murder then?'

Harris did not respond to the comment.

'I know that silence,' said Gallagher. 'You've had one of your ideas, haven't you?'

'Might have,' said Harris. His desk phone rang. 'I'll ring you back.'

He was grateful of the interruption before he found himself giving voice to a theory which, although it had been helped by his visit to Dark Waters, he did not feel was yet well-enough formed to share with colleagues. The inspector picked up the receiver.

'DCI Harris,' he said.

'It's Leckie. Our anonymous informant has just been on the blower. The AFA have been told that Ronny Carroll is still hiding out on the Langdon Estate and they have decided to go after him tonight.'

'Citizen's arrest?'

'More like citizen's lynching, I fear. Apparently, Guy Robertson is talking big about carrying out retribution for the murder of Carl Bradby. I hate to think what will happen if he and his cronies get hold of Ronny Carroll and Sebastian de la Roche.'

'I suppose we'll have to ride to the rescue. What time is all this going to happen?' asked Harris.

'Midnight.'

'Do you want to be there?'

'Sure do.'

'See you later then,' said Harris. He rang Gallagher back. 'The AFA are going after Ronny Carroll tonight. If you want to be involved, you'll have to move quickly.'

'Wouldn't miss it for the world,' said Gallagher. 'We're on our way.'

Harris headed for Gillian Roberts' office with a lightness of step. He was calling the shots again and enjoying the experience. The detective inspector, who was sitting at her desk, looked up from her paperwork when her boss entered the room.

'Who are you?' she asked.

'Sorry about that,' said Harris. 'I came to suggest that you prepare yourself for a late night.'

'Not another one?' said Roberts. She gave him a bleak look.

'I am afraid so. The AFA reckon Ronny Carroll is still on the Langdon Estate and are going after him. We need to get a team together, including the Firearms Unit. Can I leave you to sort that?'

'Sure.'

Harris headed off to see the divisional commander.

'The prodigal returns,' said Curtis, gesturing for him to take a seat.

'Sorry I've been away so long,' said Harris. 'However, I hear that you've been doing a sterling job in my absence, showing me how to run a press conference without pissing anyone off?'

'Something like that,' said Curtis. He gave the inspector a rueful look. 'Hopefully, the AFA will let it go.'

'I wouldn't bet on it, sir. Last I heard, your friendly neighbourhood deranged lunatics were on their way up here.'

Curtis looked worried.

'Not gunning for me, I hope,' he said.

'If they are, it'll only be after they have done over La Roche and his odious water bailiff,' said Harris.

* * *

The inspector had just entered his office and sat down at his desk when there was a knock on the door and Alison Butterfield walked into the room. Harris gestured for her to take a seat.

'I think I owe you an apology,' she said as she sat down.

'I think you probably do. How many times have I told you that, however boring routine police work may be, it is also vital? It's the lesson that the best officers learn first and if you had learned it, we would have turned up Carl Bradby's answering machine.'

'Yes, guv, sorry. If it helps, I've have tracked it down now.'

'Really? How did you do that?'

'Good old-fashioned police work,' she said, with a slight smile, unable to resist the opportunity.

Harris let the quip go.

'Where was it?' he asked.

'I found a list of people renting out office space in Peterborough and worked my way down it,' continued Butterfield. 'Carl Bradby was number seventeen. He didn't rent an office, just a hot desk, which was why we were having so much trouble finding it. The local police found the owner of the building and they're getting the machine sent up by courier. Oh, and I gave the phone company the hard word and I have his landline records. I'm working my way through them now.'

Harris nodded his approval.

'Excellent work, Constable,' he said.

'That's not all,' said Butterfield. Her confidence was growing by the second. 'That's why I came to see you. After it emerged that Carl Bradby had a girlfriend, I decided to recheck the background information that the

Langdon Estate provided on its people. Just in case we had missed something.'

'Sounds like boring routine police work to me,' said Harris, with a wry smile. 'Do I take it that you have found something interesting? Oh, please tell me that you have, given the fuss that La Roche made about handing the information over.'

'Well, it's a coincidence, if nothing else,' said Butterfield. 'And you always say that you don't believe in coincidences in murder investigations.'

Harris nodded.

'This one concerns Danny Brewster's pal in the office,' said Butterfield. 'Janice Garvey's CV said she arrived at the Langdon Estate five months ago, having previously worked at a fishing tackle shop in Sheffield. She moved up here to be nearer her elderly parents.'

'Nothing suspicious there, surely?' said Harris.

'No, but whichever one of our people checked her CV overlooked the fact that she had only worked in the Sheffield shop for two months, so I rang the owner. It was a long shot but you never know.'

'You never do,' said Harris. He was enjoying her enthusiasm for routine police work. 'What did you find?'

'Nothing sinister but it turns out that she came to them from another fishing tackle shop and this one was in Peterborough, which put her there at the same time as Carl Bradby. What if she is his mystery girlfriend? Maybe she found out that Dark Waters was looking for an investigator to look at the setting of snares and tipped him off?'

'It's certainly worth asking the question,' said Harris. He gave her a nod of approval. 'Good work, Constable. Do the Peterborough people remember if she had a boyfriend?'

'Unfortunately not, and I didn't want to talk to Janice about it until I'd cleared it with you, given all the politics that surrounds the Langdon Estate. Especially if it turns out to be nothing.'

'Very wise,' said Harris. 'You have my permission to look into it.'

'Thank you,' she said. An anxious look crossed her face. 'Will I still be disciplined for not tracking down the answering machine earlier?'

'I think not. No, as far as I'm concerned, you're a young officer who is finding her way,' said Harris. 'Throwing the book at you at this stage of your career would achieve little. No, I actually think you deserve a reward for all your efforts.'

'Guv?'

'It would appear that the AFA think Public Enemy Number One Ronny Carroll is still hunkering down somewhere on the Langdon Estate and they're going after him tonight. We're going to be there waiting for them. I take it that you would like to be involved?'

Butterfield opened her mouth to reply.

'Don't tell me,' said Harris. 'You wouldn't miss it for the world!'

Chapter twenty-five

The main approach to the Langdon Estate was a gravel drive which snaked its way through mature native woodland and was lined with rhododendron bushes. After a mile, the road delivered visitors to a set of ornate wrought-iron gates fitted with an intercom that allowed them to alert the office staff to their presence. The thirty-strong police team arrived shortly after 10:00pm after being given grudging permission to enter the site by Sebastian de la Roche. Despite the fact that their presence represented the protection that the estate owner had requested, he seemed determined to make things as difficult as possible, and he'd bridled at the suggestion that Ronny Carroll was still on the site, and refused to speak to Jack Harris.

La Roche's mood remained aggressive and resentful during difficult discussions with Philip Curtis but agreement was finally reached and now, with midnight approaching, a dozen officers led by Detective Inspector Gillian Roberts and including a firearms team, had based themselves in the outbuildings at the heart of the estate, with another group hiding in among the trees behind La Roche's house, the officers stamping their feet to keep warm in the deepening chill of the night. Harris and Leckie waited in the inspector's Land Rover, which was invisible as it sat in among the thick woodland close to the front gate. Scoot and Archie were in the back, as usual. Matty Gallagher had parked his car nearby. He and Alistair Marshall had arrived half an hour after everyone else, eager and bright-eyed as the rush of adrenaline created by anticipation of the night's action banished the fatigue of their frustrating experience in Scotland.

Silence settled on the Land Rover, with Harris sitting with his eyes closed and Leckie staring out into the darkness and enjoying the rare opportunity to be out in the field. The silence was broken at two minutes before midnight when the inspector wound down his window so that the officers could hear the sound of the distant hum of engines carried on the still night air.

'Looks like your informant was spot on,' said Harris.

'He usually is,' replied Leckie. 'And you're pretty sure that you know who he is? This Brewster kid?'

'I certainly think that he's the one leaking stuff about the Langdon Estate. Whoever gave Stuart Liversedge the low-down on the snares has to be someone on the inside, and because whoever did it used a fake Facebook ID, they have to be tech-savvy. Danny's the only member of staff who fits the bill, as far as we can see.'

'But you still don't know why he's doing it?' asked Leckie.

'No, and that's the problem,' said Harris with a frown. 'Danny comes from a family of keen anglers. His dad has won a couple of coarse fishing competitions and his uncle holds the record for the biggest trout ever caught on the River Nare. You might have seen the picture in the *Angling Times* last year?'

'That was his uncle, was it?' said Leckie. 'A very impressive fish. I wish I could catch one that big. So why would a kid from a family like that do everything in his power to sabotage a fishing estate?'

'I'm not sure.'

'Rebellious teenager?' suggested Leckie. He gave his friend a sly look. 'You'd know all about that.'

'Yes, thank you,' said Harris, feigning protest. His radio crackled. 'Harris.'

'Alistair here,' said a voice in the darkness. 'A motorbike has just passed us. It should be with you in a couple of minutes. Looks liked it's being ridden by a young man.'

'I suspect that's young Danny,' said Harris. 'He rides a motorbike. Excellent.'

It did not take long for the bike to arrive at the gates, where the rider dismounted and removed his crash helmet, reached into the storage pannier and produced a baseball cap, which he jammed onto his head.

'That him?' asked Leckie.

'Yeah, that's him,' said Harris. 'Silly boy, getting himself mixed up with this lot of hotheads.'

The inspector's radio crackled once more.

'Alistair here again,' said the detective constable's voice. 'Two cars have just passed us. It looks like four people in each one and they all appear to be wearing masks.'

Two sets of headlights soon pierced the darkness as the cars passed by the Land Rover's hiding place and arrived at the gates, drawing to a halt next to the motorbike with their engines running. One of the front-seat passengers got out, wearing a balaclava mask and gripping a baseball bat.

'This lot look like they mean business,' said Leckie.

'So do we,' said Harris.

After a brief conversation between the two men, there was a clanking sound as Danny Brewster unlocked the gates and the other man gave him a pat on the shoulder and returned to his car. The vehicles drove through the gate and headed along the drive in the direction of the estate. Brewster had just started to close the gates when he saw Harris and Leckie emerge from among the trees and walk purposefully towards him.

'What the—' he exclaimed but his voice tailed off as he recognised Harris and the colour drained from what the detectives could see of his features beneath the cap.

'Don't tell me,' said Harris affably. 'Sebastian de la Roche wants some nice night shots of the river for the website?'

Brewster gave him a sick look and leaned weakly against one of the gateposts.

'How did you know we would be here?' he asked after a few moments.

'Aren't you the one who tipped us off?' asked Leckie, holding up his warrant card bearing the Greater Manchester Police logo. 'The one who keeps ringing us up with information?'

'Not me,' said Brewster. 'I'm not exactly a great fan of the police.'

'Fan or not, would you care to explain what your pals are doing here?' asked Harris. 'We heard that they are after Ronny Carroll.'

'I'm saying nowt,' said Brewster. 'You're too late anyway. They'll have done it by the time you get there.'

'I think you'll find that we are a touch savvier than that,' said Harris with a thin smile. 'We have firearms officers surrounding the house.'

Brewster gave a crooked smile.

'But the AFA are not going to the house,' he said.

'What?' said Harris. He felt a knot forming in his stomach.

'They're not going to the house,' said Brewster, enjoying the shift in control of the situation. 'Ronny's not there.'

'Then where is he?' said Harris.

'You'll have to find that out for yourself,' said Brewster. 'Not even La Roche knows that he's here. He thinks that Ronny left the estate a couple of days ago.'

Before the detectives could continue with their search for answers, the scene was illuminated by headlights as a car sped down the drive and ground to a halt, throwing up pieces of gravel. Gallagher wound down the driver's window.

'What's happening?' he said.

'I'm not quite sure,' said Harris. He gestured at Brewster. 'Arrest him, will you? Take him to the office and see if you can get him to tell you where Ronny Carroll is.'

Gallagher got out, took hold of Brewster, and led him to the car, where Alistair Marshall helped him into the back seat. Harris and Leckie walked quickly back towards the Land Rover and were almost at the vehicle when the inspector's radio burst into life again. This time, the detectives could hear shouting in the background.

'Gillian here,' said the detective inspector. There was an urgency in her voice and she sounded short of breath; they guessed that she was running. 'They're not heading for the house.'

'Yeah, I know. Any idea where they might be heading?' asked Harris.

'They've turned off onto a side track. There's a ruined cottage in the wood. It used to be the water bailiff's home but it's been abandoned since part of the roof caved in following a storm in the seventies. I reckon they're heading there.'

'Hasn't it been searched?' asked Harris as he and Leckie reached the Land Rover.

'Twice,' said Roberts. 'Ronny must have been hiding out somewhere else then went back. We'll check it out.'

'We'll meet you there,' said Harris, firing up the Land Rover's engine.

Soon the two friends were driving along a rough track, the vehicle bumping over the pitted surface as they headed for the ruined house. An ominous sight greeted them when they arrived. The activists, most of whom were armed with baseball bats, had surrounded the ramshackle cottage and were yelling profanities in the direction of the man whose wide-eyed face stared out through one of the cracked windows.

'Ronny Carroll?' asked Leckie.

'Yeah,' said Harris. He noticed that one of the protestors was holding a petrol can. 'And it looks like they are going to burn the bastard out!'

He slammed his foot on the brake and wrenched on the steering wheel, and the Land Rover came to a juddering halt. As Harris and Leckie jumped out of the vehicle, a couple of the masked men turned to face them, brandishing their baseball bats.

'Stay back!' shouted one of them. 'Just fucking stay back or I'll have you!'

Harris hesitated for a moment as the two men faced up to each other, then there came a whooshing sound and the cottage burst into flames. Detectives and animal rights protestors turned instinctively to watch as Ronny Carroll gave a cry of alarm and burst through the front door of the building, followed by his terrified dog. Harris's quarry took advantage of the distraction, raised his bat and lunged at the inspector but Harris was too quick for him and lashed out with a meaty fist, which caught his assailant by surprise as it slammed into his stomach. The man gave a squeal of pain and doubled over clutching his gut, he rolled onto his side and retched violently. Harris reached down and ripped off the man's mask to reveal the unshaven features that confirmed it was Guy Robertson. Leckie clapped his hands once.

'Bravo,' he said. 'Bravo, indeed, my friend. He's had that coming for a long time.'

'I thank you,' said Harris. He gave a little bow then looked down at Robertson. 'That was for the two fishermen in Manchester.'

Harris turned to face the second masked man, who was standing transfixed as he watched Robertson lie moaning on the floor, with his face twisted in pain and spittle glistening on his lips.

'Would you like to try your luck, pal?' asked the inspector. 'There's plenty more where that came from.'

The man hesitated and took another look at the twisted face of his friend. He shook his head, turned and started to run but he did not get far because the scene was illuminated by the headlights from several police vehicles, officers on foot also converged on the scene from all sides and within seconds he had been arrested. The officers who had just arrived included the young detective constables Alison Butterfield and Sally Orr, who gave chase as one of the other protestors fled into the wood. More fleet of foot than her younger colleague, Butterfield was the first to catch up with the vigilante and hurled herself into a flying rugby tackle, grabbing her quarry's legs. The impact brought the activist crashing to the ground to writhe in pain.

Jack Harris had followed proceedings with an indulgent smile on his face.

'Good work, Constable,' said Harris. 'Let's find out who it is, shall we?'

Butterfield grinned, helped the protestor struggle to their feet and removed the mask.

'Miriam Coles, as I live and breathe,' said Harris cheerfully, as the group's co-founder glared balefully at him. The inspector looked across at Leckie. 'I wonder what a nice middle-class girl like her is doing in a place like this, Graham? I suspect she'll have a problem wheedling herself out of trouble on this one.'

'I reckon so,' said Leckie with an expression of satisfaction. His team's failure to bring members of the Anti-Fishing Alliance before a court had been irritating him for months and, even though credit for the arrests would largely go to another force, the constable felt a profound sense of a job well done. 'And it's difficult to see how the AFA can continue after this debacle.'

Coles said nothing, partly because she was still struggling to catch her breath, and partly because she knew that he was right. A warning shout diverted everyone's attention and they turned to see the remainder of the activists drop their bats and hold out their hands so that the firearms officers could ensure that they were not carrying any more weapons.

A movement over to the right caught Harris's attention and he watched Matty Gallagher chase after the fleeing Ronny Carroll. Realising that he was not going to outrun the detective, the water bailiff turned and lashed out at the sergeant with his walking stick. Harris looked on in surprise as Gallagher swayed out of the way of the stick, showing an agility that he rarely displayed, then gave an enraged roar which had built up deep inside him for many months, and snapped out a fist. The punch caught Ronny Carroll on the side of the head, sending him staggering sideways to collide with a tree and slump to the ground.

The bailiff's dog, Rasp, gave a growl and ran towards the sergeant, who scowled at the animal and, watched in amusement by his boss, flipped out a foot to send the creature careering backwards, emitting a yelp more of outrage than pain.

Recovering quickly, Rasp jumped back to his feet and made as if to launch an attack of his own. Growling in a menacing fashion, his eyes flashing with fury and his lips bared to display crooked teeth which oozed saliva. Rather than being frightened by the dog's response, Gallagher gave a fearsome growl of his own and ran towards the dog, waving his arms. Having never encountered such a response from a human, the dog stood his ground for a few moments then turned tail and fled, howling, into the night. Jack Harris roared with laughter.

'I hope he never applies for a job in the dog unit,' said Leckie.

Gallagher slapped handcuffs on Carroll's wrists and handed him to a uniformed officer then walked across to Harris and Leckie and gave a broad smile.

'I enjoyed that,' he said. 'Been wanting to lock the bastard up for ages.'

'So I noticed,' replied Harris, still chuckling.

As the various prisoners were led back down the track towards waiting police vehicles, Harris noticed that Sebastian de la Roche was heading towards him.

'Ah, good evening, Sebastian,' he said affably. 'Enough police protection for you?'

The estate owner did not reply but instead stood in silence and watched with a glum expression on his face as the fire in the cottage began to take hold and flames shot into the night air. He noticed the uniformed officer walking Ronny Carroll towards a police vehicle, followed by the disconsolate Rasp, whose limp appeared worse than ever.

'I know you won't believe me,' said La Roche. 'But I didn't know that Ronny was here.'

'Actually, I'm feeling generous,' said Harris. 'So, I do believe you.'

'Will he be charged with anything?' asked La Roche.

'Assaulting a police officer, maybe,' said the inspector. 'But not in connection with the death of Carl Bradby. Neither will you, either. No, for that we have to look elsewhere.'

'So, do you know who did it?' asked La Roche.

'All in good time,' said Harris. 'But looks like you and Ronny are in the clear.'

La Roche gave the inspector a look of approval and walked away to catch up with Carroll. Gallagher waited until he was out of earshot and gave his boss a questioning look.

'So, who did kill Carl?' he asked.

'All will become clear in due course.'

'I hate it when you act all mysterious,' said the sergeant.

Chapter twenty-six

With the trouble having been quelled in the wood, and all the intruders taken into custody, Harris drove the Land Rover to the main estate yard, where he found Gillian Roberts overseeing the loading of the prisoners into police vans. They appeared stunned by the events that had unfolded and Harris congratulated the detective inspector her on a well-planned operation before taking the opportunity to talk to Danny Brewster before he was taken to Levton Bridge Police Station for further questioning.

The inspector took Brewster to the office where the young man sat down and eyed the detective with an increasingly anxious look on his face as the enormity of his situation became ever more apparent. Harris remained standing and looked down at him.

'How come it's just you and me?' asked Brewster nervously. 'You're not going to beat me up, are you?'

'Beat you up? Why on earth would I do that, Danny?'

'I saw what you did to Guy Robertson out there. And I've heard the stories about you. That you don't mind roughing people up.'

'Yes, well, you shouldn't believe every story you hear,' said Harris. 'They're not true.'

Brewster relaxed.

'Well, most of them aren't, anyway,' added Harris mischievously. He chuckled at Brewster's look of alarm. 'Don't look so worried, son. There really is nothing to be concerned about as long as you're co-operative.'

'Then how come I'm not being taken into town with the others?' asked Brewster.

'That will happen in due course but before that I want to talk to you about the murder of Carl Bradby.'

'That's nothing to do with me!' protested Brewster. The sweat glistening on his forehead and his trembling right hand stood testament to the acute emotions that he was experiencing. 'I never even met him!'

'I didn't say you did.'

'Then why are you asking me about him? Shouldn't I have a lawyer?'

'You can have one tomorrow, if you really want one,' said Harris. 'But, for now, Danny, this is unofficial – just a chat. Let me try to put your mind at rest. We know that you're not like the members of the AFA. I suspect we'll end up charging them with affray but that won't happen to you. In fact, I'm not sure you will be charged with anything. Off-hand, I can't think what law you have broken, at least not until they make the naivety of youth illegal.'

Brewster looked relieved.

'However,' said Harris, 'you might be able to help us with our inquiries into the murder. You told my colleague from Greater Manchester Police earlier tonight that you are not the person who has been anonymously passing on information about the AFA to his officers.'

'Yeah, that's right, I'm not.'

'But, presumably, you *are* the person who has been passing anonymous information on to the AFA themselves?'

'No, that's not me either,' said Brewster.

'Then how come you opened the gates for them tonight?'

'Because Stuart Liversedge asked me to. I told him that I'd heard that Ronny was still hiding out on the estate. He got back in touch with me and said that the AFA were coming for Ronny and that, if I knew what was good for me, I would let them in.'

'Why choose you to open the gates?' asked Harris. 'There's nigh on twenty people working here. Why not ask someone else?'

'Because I was the one who told him about the snares.'

'But he told us that he didn't know who you were,' said Harris. 'He said that you passed on information from an account with a fake ID. Are you telling me that he knew it was you all along?'

'He might have guessed, I suppose, but, if he did, he never said. I just made sure that he could message me back, if he wanted.'

'Were you passing information on to anyone else?' asked Harris. 'Sebastian de la Roche, maybe?'

'No.'

'What about Scotland?' asked Harris. 'Have you passed information to anyone up there?'

'Why would I do that?' Brewster gave him a suspicious look. 'What's this about, anyway? And what's it got to do with the murder?'

'I am trying to get my head round all the information that has been circulating. Trying to work out where it has been coming from.'

'Is it important?'

'It could be,' said Harris. 'Have you ever heard of the Probert brothers?'

'Like I keep telling you, I only give information about the estate to Stuart. What he does with it is up to him. I don't give anything to anyone else.'

'Why do it at all?' asked Harris. 'You've hardly shown much loyalty to your employer, have you?'

'Him!' said Brewster vehemently. 'He doesn't deserve it! And I'm not ashamed of what I did, neither. I know that some people might say that it cost Carl Bradby his life but someone had to stop the snares being set. Have you seen an animal that has died in one, Chief Inspector?'

'I have, and you'll get no argument from me on banning the things, but you come from a big fishing family,' said Harris. 'I would have thought that you would be pro the sport.'

'Working here has changed the way I think about it,' said Brewster. 'And it's not just the snares, either. Seeing the way that Ronny deals with the fish in the ponds, knocking them about, leaving the injured ones to die on the path, gasping for air, then listening to La Roche banging on about culling otters – they were some of the reasons I changed my opinion. It made me feel sick.'

'Were there any other reasons?' asked Harris.

'I met this girl.'

'Ah, of course you did,' said Harris with a slight smile. 'So much for strongly held principle, eh, Danny? I should have guessed that it came down to the basest of instincts. It usually does. This girl is not a fan of fishing, I take it?'

'She was horrified when I told her what this place was like. She's not an animal rights activist, not like them in the AFA, but she does care and I started to worry that she might drop me, so I decided to show her that I cared. Get into her good books.'

'Is that all you wanted to get into?'

'That's not fair,' said Brewster. 'I genuinely wanted to do something to stop people like La Roche and Ronny Carroll getting away with all the cruelty.'

'Amen to that,' said Harris. He stood up and headed for the door. 'Oh, one last thing. We've been told that Carl Bradby had a girlfriend. I don't suppose you know anything about her?'

'Sorry,' said Brewster, 'it's the first I have heard about it.'

Harris gave him a hard look.

'Are you sure?' he said.

'Yes, I'm sure. Why do you want to know about his girlfriend, anyway?'

'Oh, just idle curiosity,' said Harris.

Chapter twenty-seven

Following the events at the Langdon Estate, Harris and Leckie went back to the inspector's cottage and managed to grab a few hours of fitful sleep. The inspector woke first, just after six, which was late for him, and, having left his friend to slumber, he fed the dogs then took them for a walk across the hillside. When man and beasts returned to the cottage, it was to be greeted by the tantalising aroma of frying bacon as Leckie prepared breakfast. Having eaten their meal, the inspector loaded Scoot and Archie into the back of the Land Rover and Harris set the vehicle rattling and rolling along the bumpy track that led down to the main valley road.

They reached Levton Bridge Police Station just before 8:30am and entered a building that was much quieter than the one at the centre of the hubbub the previous night, which had been filled with the loud hollering of protest and the slamming of feet against cell doors as the animal rights activists were taken into custody. As Harris checked in with members of his team and Leckie rang colleagues in Manchester to update them on developments, Scoot and Archie busied themselves in conducting their customary morning trot around the station, giving their usual morning greetings to favoured staff and receiving treats in return.

With his checks complete, Harris headed out to the front of the building and stood at the top of the steps to talk to the assembled media, who had gathered following the issue of a press release giving some details about the events at the Langdon Estate. With his briefing completed, the inspector turned and headed for the front door, appearing determined to refuse to answer the journalists' questions, as usual. However, something made him change his mind and, to the journalists' surprise, he turned back and answered questions for ten minutes before making his way into the police station, leaving the bewildered representatives of the media to debate what they had just witnessed. As he pushed open the door into reception, Harris paused for a moment and listened to the journalists' discussion. Harris 1 – Curtis 0, he thought.

When he was back inside the station, he headed for the custody suite where the noise level was on the rise again as several of the animal rights activists started to yell profanities, shouting which grew louder when they realised that Harris had arrived. Ignoring them, he headed for the cell containing Miriam Coles, who remained outwardly calm despite the clamour about her.

'If it's not the legendary Jack Harris,' she said. There was a tinge of mockery in her voice. 'I suppose you're proud of yourself, are you? Using the Fascist Police State complete with guns to silence the legitimate voice of public protest?'

'You can knock the left-wing claptrap on the head,' replied Harris, leaning against the wall. 'And as for "the legitimate voice of public protest", it tends not, from my experience, to come with baseball bats and cans of petrol.'

'Sometimes it's the only way to make people listen. I take it that you will be the one who interviews me when my solicitor arrives?'

'No, it'll be Detective Inspector Roberts. I've got more important things to do,' said Harris. He gave a slight smile as he saw her scowl; he knew that she had a reputation for being irritated by anyone who suggested that the AFA was an irrelevance. 'I do have one question for you, though.'

Coles looked at him suspiciously.

'Shouldn't we be in an interview room with the tape running and my solicitor present?' she asked.

'The Fascist Police State tends not to operate that way.'

'You really are full of yourself, aren't you?' she said. 'What's your question, anyway?'

'It relates to the information you have received, particularly over the past couple of weeks, tip-offs about events on the Langdon Estate, the inside track on police investigations, that sort of thing. Where does it come from? I'm not asking for names, just how you receive it.'

Coles hesitated. The question had surprised her but, for all she was wary of the police, she could not see any harm in answering it.

'I wouldn't give you the names even if I knew them,' she said. 'But, as it happens, I don't. Our information comes mainly in the form of anonymous tip-offs. I have no idea who they are from, or even how many of them there are. They send emails we can't track and disguise their voices.'

'Thank you,' said Harris, heading for the door.

'Is that it?' she asked, looking confused.

'It is,' said the inspector. 'I'll send a couple of fascists in a little later to give you a good kicking. You have a nice day now.'

Once in the corridor with the cell door closed, Harris took his mobile phone out of his jacket pocket and rang Gallagher.

'Matty lad,' he said. 'We need to go back to Scotland. Do you fancy coming along for the ride?'

'I thought we had ruled the Proberts out?'

'And so we have,' said Harris. 'But I think I know who our murderer is.'

'Who is it?'

'Stuart Liversedge,' said Harris dramatically.

'Well, it might be possible.'

'You don't sound surprised,' said Harris. He was unable to hide the disappointment in his voice; he had assumed that the sergeant would be impressed by his naming of someone who had not featured as a suspect in their discussions.

'Let's just say that it's not a complete shock,' said Gallagher. He was enjoying the effect that his deadpan response was having on his boss. 'If you pop along to the squad room, we can explain.'

A couple of minutes later, the inspector was standing in the squad room with Gallagher, Gillian Roberts and Alison Butterfield, all looking at a telephone answering machine sitting on one of the desks.

'That's Carl Bradby's machine, I take it?' said Harris. He leaned closer to get a better look. 'I assume that you've turned something up on the messages?'

'We have,' said Gallagher. 'Possibly, starting with the identity of Carl Bradby's girlfriend.'

Harris glanced at Butterfield.

'Did you not tell them that we are going to look closer at Janice Garvey?' he said. 'I forgot to mention it, what with everything that was going on last night.'

'It may not be that simple,' said the constable. She picked up her notebook from the desk and referred to one of the pages. 'You'll find out why when we get to the last three messages. Before that comes four messages from people who wanted to see if he could do any work for them, and one from his accountant. Then there are the calls from the young lad you met in Scotland. Luke McAllister.'

'They would seem to confirm that he was telling the truth about his relationship with Bradby,' said Gallagher.

'But it's another relationship that is interesting us, the one with the woman in Carl's life.'

Gallagher looked at the answering machine.

'These are the final three messages,' he said. 'They were all left in recent days.'

The sergeant pressed a button and they heard a woman's voice.

'It's me,' she said in a voice that sounded anxious.

Harris gave a look of surprise.

'That's Anna Liversedge,' he said.

'Sure is,' said Gallagher.

'I can't get a reply from your mobile,' continued Anna. 'I think it's switched off. Ring me as soon as you get this, will you?'

Harris was about to say something when there was a beeping noise from the machine and the next message came on. This time, Anna seemed close to tears.

'I hope you get this message,' she said. 'A body has been found on the riverbank near the Langdon Estate and I am terrified that it's you. Ring me if you get this.'

There was another beep and the final message came on. This time, Anna's voice was quiet and shaking, and the listening detectives found it difficult to decipher what she was saying through the tears that threatened to overwhelm her.

'The police still haven't named the person on the riverbank,' she sobbed. 'But Stuart says that he's sure it must be you and I still can't get an answer from your mobile and...'

And there the message ended.

'It could be innocent,' said Harris. 'Checking on the welfare of someone that Dark Waters hired?'

'Except I got the impression that Stuart dealt with the investigators,' said Gallagher. 'And yet here is Anna leaving three messages for Carl Bradby in a short time frame. We are wondering if Stuart found out that Carl Bradley was in a relationship with his wife – or maybe he got it into head they were having an affair – and killed him. A good old-fashioned tale of jealousy.'

'I had him top of my list for another reason,' said Harris, 'but I guess I should not be too surprised. Like I told Danny Brewster last night, it's remarkable how often investigations that look complicated actually come down to base instinct…'

Chapter twenty-eight

'If you didn't identify Stuart Liversedge as a murder suspect through his wife's affair, how on earth did you come to think that it was him?' asked Gallagher.

He glanced across at Harris, who was driving the Land Rover through the outskirts of Levton Bridge and onto the beginnings off the moorland road that would lead them to the northbound M6.

'It only really started to come together when I saw him yesterday,' said the inspector. 'And my suspicions were strengthened when I talked to Danny Brewster and Miriam Coles. I briefly considered Danny as the murderer, actually.'

'Surely, you didn't think that he could be capable of killing someone?'

'Anyone is capable of taking a life, Matty lad, you've been a police officer long enough to know that. And Danny *was* close to the riverbank the day Bradby was killed, remember.'

'Yeah, but can you really see him getting the best of an ex-SAS man?'

'No, which is why he was only a passing thought,' said Harris. 'I was more interested in him because he's well connected. Finding someone like that was the key.'

'What do you mean?' asked Gallagher. 'None of this made sense until the answering machine turned up. Things just kept getting more confusing.'

'I suspect that was the intention all along,' said Harris.

'You make it sound like someone orchestrated the whole thing.'

'Orchestrated is an excellent word to describe it, Matty lad. Do you recall our conversation a couple of days ago when I admitted that I had been making mistakes?'

Gallagher nodded.

'Well, when I was with Greater Manchester Police, I used to run training courses for detectives and would tell them that a good investigator should consider all the options but that there must come a time when they focus in on the most likely scenario. My biggest mistake on this investigation has been allowing myself to be distracted but once I focused on the most likely scenario, the more I became convinced that one individual had created all the confusion to ensure that we did not look in their direction for the murder.'

The inspector stopped talking for a moment as he applied the brakes and changed down a gear to allow the Land Rover to negotiate a sharp bend and begin the steep climb up onto the moor.

'And you decided Stuart was that person?' said Gallagher.

'The more I thought about it, the more obvious it became,' said Harris. 'He sits at the centre of things. Who had us so distracted that we ended up running off to Scotland? Then when I told him last night that we were no longer interested in the brothers, he was at it again. He said that he had become convinced that Ronny killed Carl Bradby and was responsible for the attacks on the Dark Waters property, attacks which I suspect he faked to make him look like a victim. And for good measure last night, he also told me about the AFA's planned attack on the Langdon Estate and suggested that they are perfectly capable of murder. Mix into that all the anonymous tip-offs to Greater Manchester Police, the AFA and the Langdon Estate, which I suspect were also down to him, and what do you get? Distraction after distraction, an ever-lengthening list of suspects, a confused CID team, a detective chief inspector who has lost his focus and so much high emotion that no one is thinking straight. It's quite elegant, in its own way.'

'And all to hide the fact that he killed Carl?' said Gallagher.

'That's what I think,' said the inspector. He changed up another gear as the Land Rover reached the summit of its climb and emerged onto the vast expanse of moorland. 'The problem was that I didn't have a motive until the answering machine turned up. I'd heard nothing to suggest that Anna was having an affair but when you played the messages, it seemed to make sense. You may have been spot on when you said that it all comes down to good old-fashioned jealousy. It's one of the oldest motives in the book, after all.'

'It is,' said Gallagher. 'Do you think Anna knows that her husband killed Bradby?'

'I suspect not. She was very upset last night but that was probably because her husband has convinced her that Dark Waters is under siege from a deranged Ronny Carroll with his shotgun. *I'd* be frightened.'

'So, what's the plan? Arrest Stuart and bring him back to Levton Bridge?'

Harris nodded.

'Maureen Strothers has offered us back-up if we need it,' he said. 'But I told her that we'd be OK. I am pretty sure he does not know that we're onto him.'

'Don't you think it would be a good idea to have one or two bodies to support us anyway?' said Gallagher. 'I mean, if you're right that Stuart faked the attacks, it means that he has a shotgun, doesn't it. Who knows how he will react when we bowl in there waggling our warrant cards?'

'Except he still thinks we're on his side so he's unlikely to do anything. We've got the element of surprise so by the time he works out what's happening, we'll have arrested him. If we turn up with firearms back-up, he'll guess why we're there and things could escalate.'

Harris noticed Gallagher frowning.

'It'll be fine,' said the inspector. 'Trust me, Matty lad.'

* * *

They were well into their journey when the inspector's mobile phone rang. Harris leaned over to see who was calling.

'It's the DI,' he said. 'I ran my theory past her and asked her to check with Northumbria Police that Anna reached her sister's house alright last night. Just in case. I'm sure she's fine. Like I said, Stuart has no idea that we're onto him.'

The inspector's confidence was dispelled by the anxiety in Roberts' voice.

'It looks like we've been spun a line,' she said. 'Northumbria Police have just been on. They sent a couple of officers to Craster but the sister's house is empty. They talked to the neighbours and she's away on holiday for a fortnight. Went six days ago. There's no sign of Anna.'

'That's worrying,' said Harris.

'Maybe we do need that armed back-up when we arrest Stuart, after all,' said Gallagher.

'It might be a good idea,' said Roberts. 'After you ran your theory past me, Jack, I had a word with Maureen and their firearms licensing people have confirmed that Stuart Liversedge does have a shotgun. I think you're right that he faked the attacks on Dark Waters to make him look like a victim. I certainly don't think that it's anything to do with

Ronny Carroll and I never thought I'd find myself standing up for the old rogue.'

'A low point in an otherwise glorious police career,' said Harris.

'Something like that,' said Roberts. 'Except for the "glorious" bit. Anyway, I've just been to see Ronny in his cell and, rather predictably, he denied that he was the one who shot at Stuart but, like I say, I tend to believe him. I asked around and no one can remember having ever seen him with a shotgun and our firearms licensing people said that they don't think he has ever had one. There's certainly no record of it. It's not looking good for Stuart Liversedge.'

'No, it's not,' said Harris. His phone vibrated and he glanced at the notification box. 'I'm going to have to go, Gillian, I've got Maureen on the phone.'

The inspector took the call. The drone of a car engine in the background told the Levton Bridge detectives that Maureen Strothers was on the road.

'I was just going to ring you,' said Harris. 'Gillian told me what you said about Liversedge having a shotgun so I think we're going to say yes to that offer of armed back-up. It looks like Anna Liversedge didn't get to her sister's last night and I'm beginning to get this nasty feeling that she may have come to some harm.'

'So am I,' said Strothers. 'Particularly when you hear what we've found out about her husband. After you told me that he was a suspect, I asked one of our intelligence people to check the records to see if we have anything on the Liversedges. Just on the off-chance. I didn't expect to find anything but it turns out that Stuart has received two police cautions for threatening Anna over the past five years.'

'Brilliant,' said Harris with a sigh. 'What happened?'

'The first one was in 2019 when Anna called 999 late at night and said that Stuart had drunk too much, that they had an argument and he had slapped her face. She said that she was frightened of being in the house with him but that there was nowhere to go at that time of night. Because their place is so remote, the cops did not get anyone there until gone 6:00am, by which time she had calmed down so they gave Stuart a caution and left it at that.'

'But it happened again?' said Harris.

'It did. November 2022. Same type of thing. It was her birthday and Stuart got drunk again. This time, he gave her a black eye. He was very contrite when the cops got there so they gave him another warning but told him that if it happened again, he would be charged. There's been nothing since.'

'How come no one mentioned this before?' asked Harris.

'It wasn't my team that dealt with the incidents and we had no reason to look for anything like that, given that we were dealing with bad lads dumping chemicals in rivers. However, we probably should have checked Liversedge's background as a matter of routine. Someone should definitely have told the firearms licensing people before they approved his shotgun application. It's a failure of basic police work, I am afraid.'

'I'm saying nothing,' said Harris.

'It would seem that your young constable is not the only person to have re-learned a hard lesson this week,' said Strothers.

'Indeed it would,' said Harris. 'Sounds like you're on the road. Are you heading to Dark Waters?'

'I'll be there in about an hour. There's a lay-by a couple of miles down from the site and I have told our people to meet up there. I don't want to send the first officers to arrive in on their own. Can I suggest that you meet us there as well, then we can go in together? God knows what we'll find…'

Chapter twenty-nine

What the police found when they arrived at the Dark Waters rescue centre was a surreal sight. As the officers assembled near the front gate, in the car park containing the two vehicles belonging to Stuart and Anna Liversedge, they could see that the doors to all of the aviaries had been left open, allowing the injured birds to wander unchecked along the paths.

'This does not look good,' said Harris, grim-faced as he pushed his way through the front gate. 'This does not look good at all.'

Adding to the sense of foreboding was the fact that none of the birds were making any noise, instead they were silent and with an air of confusion at their newly found freedom. Nervously following Harris as he traversed the caged areas, Strothers, Gallagher, and several uniformed officers, two of whom were carrying firearms, all felt the effect of the oppressive atmosphere and kept glancing round in search of danger. For Harris, the only sound was the pounding of his heart as he led the team along the paths and it was a relief when they reached the house, until they experienced further unease when they saw that the front door was open.

Now, the firearms officers took the lead and gestured for the others to stay back while they cautiously entered the house, advancing slowly along the hallway, weapons at the ready and shouting warnings to which there was no reply. Waiting outside the house, the other officers could hear the call of 'Clear' as each room was checked and found to be empty. After a few minutes, the firearms officers emerged back into the midday sunlight.

'There's no one here, ma'am,' said one of them. 'And no sign of a struggle or anything like that.'

'So, where are they?' asked Strothers, looking round the group.

'Wherever they are, I fear the worst for Anna,' said Gallagher.

'So what are we thinking?' asked Strothers. 'He confronts her about the affair, loses his cool, shoots her then does for himself?'

'It's certainly possible,' said Harris. 'I suspect that the birds have been let out because Stuart could not know for certain when the next people would visit. They were everything to him and he would want to make sure that they were safe. Clearly, he did not expect to live.'

'And there was no sign of any of this when you were here last night?' asked Strothers.

'Not that I saw,' said Harris. 'But I have this awful feeling that I may be partially responsible for what happened.'

'What makes you say that?'

'Because just before I left, I asked if they knew anything about Carl Bradby having a girlfriend. At that point, it had not crossed my mind that it was Anna and I did not make a big thing of it, but perhaps it sparked something after I left. There was already a tense-enough atmosphere because Stuart had convinced her that Ronny Carroll was after them with a shotgun. It would not have taken much to tip either of them over the edge, particularly Anna.'

'I don't think you can really blame yourself,' said Strothers.

'Agreed,' said Gallagher. 'You did nothing wrong, guv. So what's the next move then? Search the area?'

'I'll call in some back-up,' said Strothers, 'and I'll see if we can't get some air support as well, just in case they are alive and have gone over the hills.'

She was about to make the call when one of the uniformed officers pointed to a lone figure approaching the house along a rough track. As the figure neared them, the officers could see that it was Anna Liversedge, staring at them through lifeless eyes, as if in a trance. The sight of the officers seemed to bring her to her senses and, on realising where she was, she swayed and sunk to her knees. Strothers and Gallagher ran towards her and helped her into the house, where she lay on the sofa in the living room, her eyes closed, skin pale, breathing shallow and not answering any of their questions. It was almost as if she was not aware that anyone else was in the room with her.

Jack Harris stood and stared out of the window without speaking, brooding in silence as he replayed over and over again in his mind the events of the previous evening, trying to work out whether, if he had his time again, he would have done anything different. Whether, reassurance from colleagues or not, he had made yet another mistake. He did not come up with an answer.

Back on the hill, the uniformed officers began their search and after twenty minutes, one of the firearms team walked into the living room with a sombre expression on his face that told the detectives all that they needed to know.

'We've found him,' he said in a flat voice.

'Where was he?' asked Strothers.

'There's a duck pond just over the ridge. He was lying on the bank.'

'Dead?' asked Harris.

The firearms officer glanced at the sofa, where Anna still had her eyes closed. Strothers gave him a nod.

'Yeah, he's dead,' said the officer.

'Did you find the shotgun?' asked Harris.

'It was lying next to the body.' He looked at Anna and kept his voice low. 'He's been shot in the stomach but I think you'll want to take a look at him. You'll understand when you do.'

As the detectives made for the door, Anna opened her eyes and struggled into a sitting position.

'I tried to stop him doing it,' she said weakly, tears starting in her eyes. 'I tried to get the gun off him but he was too strong and there was nothing I could do to stop him.'

Leaving one of the uniformed officers to keep an eye on her, the three detectives accompanied the firearms officer to the pond where his colleague was standing guard over the body of Stuart Liversedge.

'See what I mean?' said the firearms officer. He pointed to the shotgun lying on the dead man's lap.

'I reckon you're right.' Harris looked back in the direction of the house. 'This investigation is twisting more than an eel in a net.'

'See,' said Gallagher. 'I said that you were poetic.'

Chapter thirty

With Harris having satisfied himself that a local Wildlife Trust was going to look after the birds from Dark Waters, he and Gallagher headed south with Anna Liversedge in the Land Rover. She said very little on the journey to Levton Bridge and continued with the monosyllabic approach when she arrived at the police station. Harris delayed the interview with her as long as he could because he was waiting for a number of crucial updates, but Anna Liversedge's solicitor kept asking for it to start and, with the clock ticking its way towards 6:30pm, Harris realised that he had run out of time and relented.

Now, Anna sat next to her solicitor in the interview room at the police station, still pale-faced and with one hand gripping the edge of table as if to keep herself upright. Harris noted the concerned looks that the lawyer kept giving her.

'I apologise that you have had to wait,' he said. 'Miss Cavanagh, our medical examiner assures me that your client is fit to be interviewed. Are you happy that we go ahead?'

Elspeth Cavanagh nodded.

'I'll help you in any way I can,' said Anna. 'I just want to get it over with.'

The exchange seemed to satisfy the lawyer, who nodded.

'Ask your questions,' she said.

'You have to believe me when I say that I didn't realise how much everything was getting to Stuart,' said Anna before either detective could speak. 'I really didn't. He's always been the strong one, the one who looked after me, and he seemed to be coping well but the attack with the shotgun was the final straw.'

Harris gave her a nod of encouragement.

'Something changed after the shots were fired at him,' said Anna. 'But I didn't realise that he was thinking of taking his own life. I just thought that he was going to the pond this morning to see if the ducks were alright and I didn't know that he had taken the shotgun. I would have gone after him if I had known. I'd have tried to stop him.'

'We'll come to that in due course,' said Harris. 'Can you just confirm one thing first, please? We believe that you had an affair with Carl Bradley. Is that correct?'

Shock flickered across Anna Liversedge's face for a moment, but only for a moment, and she quickly regained control of her responses and looked at Harris in amazement.

'An affair?' she exclaimed. 'What on earth makes you think I was having an affair?'

'Because we found Carl's answering machine,' said Harris.

'Well, then you'll have heard the messages from me.'

'We have, yes.'

'They're hardly evidence of an affair,' said Anna. She laughed. 'You really have got it wrong. Do you really think that I am the kind of woman to have an affair with a man like Carl Bradby? I was ringing him because we had heard that a body had been found on the Langdon Estate, we couldn't get an answer from his mobile phone and we were concerned that it might be him.'

'We were under the impression that Stuart dealt with the investigators?'

'Not always. Sometimes, I talked to them.'

The inspector looked at the lawyer.

'Miss Cavanagh,' he said, 'might I suggest that your client is not helping herself if we subsequently discover that she *was* having an affair with Carl Bradby, which I am pretty confident we will. Having an affair is not illegal whereas lying to the police is. Our main interest is trying to work out if her husband had a motive to kill Carl.'

'I'm sure he wouldn't do a thing like that!' exclaimed Anna.

She burst into tears.

'I wonder if I might have a moment with my client in private?' asked the solicitor, viewing her with concern. 'She has been under great strain and your questions are not helping.'

'Surely,' said Harris.

The detectives left the room.

'What do you think?' asked Gallagher when they were out in the corridor.

'I think she rehearsed every word that she said,' replied Harris. 'And her ability to summon tears to order is quite remarkable.'

'So, you still fancy her for killing Stuart, do you, then? I mean, we've got precious little to go on.'

'That scene by the duck pond was staged,' said Harris. 'I'd bet my reputation on it, Matty lad. I'm just waiting for Police Scotland to send the expert testimony that proves it. And, hopefully, Gillian has got hold of those phone records. They are pretty damning. We're playing for time here, remember.'

The door to the interview room opened and Elspeth Cavanagh appeared.

'My client would like to make a statement,' she said.

The detectives returned to the room to look across the table at a composed Anna Liversedge.

'I owe you both an apology,' she said. 'You are right. I *was* having an affair. The truth is that my marriage to Stuart had been pretty meaningless for several years. He was more interested in his birds and his investigations, and I felt increasingly ignored and lonely. We had grown apart.'

'So why lie about having an affair?' asked Harris.

'An affair doesn't exactly reflect well on me, does it? Also, Stuart was very popular with our supporters and if it became common knowledge that I was cheating on him, it could have done incalculable damage to Dark Waters. People would have stopped giving us money and we rely on their donations to keep our work going.' Tears started to form in her eyes again. 'I owe Stuart at least that.'

'So, when did the relationship with Carl begin?' asked Harris.

'Not long after Stuart hired him to investigate the Proberts.' Anna's demeanour was calm now, her responses measured. 'He came to the house a couple of times and we hit it off immediately. I couldn't get him out of my mind. He was something different, exciting, someone who noticed that I existed. I was in a very vulnerable state and we started the affair a couple of weeks later. I was like a giddy teenager. I couldn't get enough of him.'

She gave them a coy smile.

'Then, of course, there was the sex,' she said. 'I'd never experienced anything like it.'

'I am assuming that you and Carl had to meet away from Dark Waters to avoid him finding out?' said Gallagher.

'Hotels, mainly,' said Anna. 'Carl's work meant he moved around a bit so it wasn't difficult.'

'But didn't your husband think it odd that you kept going away?' asked the sergeant. 'I reckon I would start to suspect that something was going on behind my back if my wife kept disappearing.'

'Stuart had long since stopped taking notice of me. I have a lot of friends and he knew that going to visit them was my way of coping with living where we do. Life in somewhere that isolated can do strange things to the mind.'

Gallagher glanced at Harris.

'I imagine it can,' he said.

Harris gave the slightest of smiles but said nothing, allowing Gallagher to continue with his line of questioning.

'So your husband did not suspect anything?' asked the sergeant.

'Carl used to say that it was easy to keep things a secret when you are going out with a former SAS man whose speciality is covert surveillance,' said Anna with a smile.

Despite the tension in the room, the detectives allowed themselves a smile at the joke. Moment of levity over, Harris glanced up at the wall clock and gave a slight frown; Maureen Strothers and Gillian Roberts should have come through with at least one of the pieces of evidence that he was waiting for. Noticing that silence had settled on the room and that everyone was waiting for him to speak, he realised that he had no option but to begin to increase the pressure on Anna Liversedge and hope that the pieces of evidence arrived in time.

'But Stuart did work it out eventually, though, didn't he?' he said, looking at her. 'I think he worked it out last night. I think that's why he's dead.'

Anna shook her head.

'You do have a vivid imagination, Chief Inspector,' she said.

* * *

In the police station's custody suit, Ronny Carroll banged on the door of his cell. It was opened by Gillian Roberts.

'What's all the noise?' she asked.

'I asked to see someone half an hour ago,' replied Carroll angrily.

'Yes, well, we're very busy, Ronny, and it may come as a shock to you to discover that you are not the only person in the world. Anyway, what do you want?'

'How come I am still being held here and all the AFA lot have gone? I've done nowt wrong. Mr de la Roche said I was the victim, so why am I still being held?'

'Jack Harris's orders,' said the detective inspector. 'He says you are not to be released until he has finished talking to Anna Liversedge.'

'She's here?' said Carroll. He sounded worried.

'The DCI and Detective Sergeant Gallagher brought her down from Scotland earlier today,' said Roberts. 'They've been interviewing her for the best part of an hour.'

'Interviewing her about what? I told you that I had nowt to do with the attacks on her home.'

'You did indeed, Ronny, but they are talking to her about something else,' said Roberts. 'The death of Carl Bradby, I believe. The DCI has got it into his head that Anna Liversedge is involved somehow.'

Carroll rubbed his unshaven chin nervously and Roberts gave the slightest of smiles; she was enjoying watching the water bailiff's anxiety grow.

'Yes, well, that's got nowt to do with me,' he said.

'Really?' said Roberts, holding up a list of telephone numbers.

'What are they?' asked Carroll uneasily.

'They,' said Roberts, 'would seem to suggest that Anna has been in regular contact with your brother and we are wondering why. Don't look so anxious. I'm sure it's nothing to worry about and that there is a perfectly innocent explanation. I imagine that the DCI will explain everything when he gets a spare minute or two.'

'Yeah, well I want to see him now.'

'I can't interrupt an interview just like that,' said Roberts. 'I have to have a good reason.'

'Tell him that it's important. Really important.'

'I will,' said Roberts. 'But I don't know if he'll come. Like I say, he's very busy.'

* * *

Harris appeared in the cell five minutes later; he was holding the telephone record. Carroll eyed it suspiciously.

'Sorry for keeping you here so long, Ronny,' he said affably. 'I meant to come to see you earlier but it's been one of those days.'

'What's that bitch been saying?' demanded Carroll. 'Has she mentioned me?'

'Anna Liversedge? Why should she mention you?' asked Harris. He tried to look as if the question had taken him by surprise. 'I wouldn't have thought that a woman like her would have wanted anything to do with a low-life like you, Ronny.'

Carroll relaxed slightly.

'It's just that DI Roberts said that you were talking about my brother,' he said. 'Something about him being in contact with Anna Liversedge.'

'Did she now?' Harris frowned. 'Well, she shouldn't really have done that, Ronny.'

The inspector feigned the pretence of someone who was thinking when he already knew that it was time to turn the screw on the water bailiff. Carroll looked increasingly worried as the silence lengthened.

'I guess that I might as well tell you,' said Harris eventually. 'You see, we'd been thinking that it was Anna's husband who killed Carl Bradby but now we know that it's not true.'

'You do?' said Carroll uneasily.

'We do, yes, so we started wondering who else might have done it and, because Carl was working for Dark Waters, we took a look at Anna's mobile phone records.'

Harris held up the piece of paper. 'And that's when we found out that she rang your brother's number several times in the days leading up to the murder. This is the brother that said he hadn't talked to you for ages. So, we went to see Davie and, lo and behold, it turns out that he had been passing messages from Anna on to you. Now why on earth would he do that, Ronny?'

Carroll looked shocked at the turn of events.

'Actually, there's no need to answer,' said Harris. He was enjoying himself. 'I reckon that when we tell Anna what we know, the whole story will come out. But she'll want to put as much distance between you and her as she can, particularly when she learns that our forensics lab has finally got round to looking at a sliver of wood that was found in Carl Bradby's skull and has concluded that it's a ninety per cent match for the posts that you used to fix the fence on the day he was murdered. If you ask me, Ronny, when Anna hears that, she'll throw you under the bus.'

'But it was her idea! Bradby told Dark Waters that he was going to be on the riverbank that morning – he needed to check out some things in daylight – and Anna told Davie where he would be. That was how I was able to hide and catch Bradby by surprise.' Carroll thought for a few moments. 'I want to make a statement.'

'I'll bet you do,' said Harris. He opened the door into the corridor. 'Sergeant, would you come in here, please?'

Gallagher appeared.

'Guv?' he said.

'I thought that, given your history with our friend here, you might be the one to caution him in connection with the murder of Carl Bradby?'

Gallagher grinned.

'Would I?' he said.

* * *

Half an hour later, as Harris and Gallagher left the interview room, with the sergeant clutching Carroll's statement, Gillian Roberts appeared in the corridor.

'Did it work?' she asked.

'Sure did,' said Harris. He gestured at the sheaf of papers in the detective inspector's hand. 'That what I think it is?'

'It certainly is,' said Gallagher.

'About time,' said Harris.

He took a couple of minutes to read the contents, gave a grunt of satisfaction and he and Gallagher returned to the interview room where Anna Liversedge was waiting with her solicitor. Anna looked at them anxiously.

'I do apologise for the interruption,' said the inspector. 'I got called away by something important. Anna, I was about to ask you what happened last night?'

She nodded at the printouts.

'What are they?' she asked.

'All in due course,' said the inspector. 'Let's go through what happened last night first, shall we? Am I right in guessing that Stuart had found out about your affair?'

Anna nodded.

'He'd been asking questions for a few days, where was I going, who was I going to see, but it was like your question last night triggered something in him,' she said. She shuddered at the memory. 'I was having second thoughts about going to my sister's – I didn't want to leave Stuart on his own – but when you had gone, he went crazy.'

'Crazy how?' asked Harris.

'You probably didn't see it but he gave me a funny look when you mentioned Carl having a girlfriend then, after you left, it was like he had lost control of his senses.' She took a few moments to regain her composure as she relived the events of the previous evening. 'He said he knew that I'd been having an affair with Carl. He said that he would teach me a lesson for being unfaithful. That's when he went for me. I thought he was going to punch me, like he did the last time he lost his temper. His right fist was clenched and he looked angry but something stopped him and he suddenly went really cold. That was more frightening than him losing his temper. That's when he confessed to killing Carl.'

'*He* said that?'

Anna nodded.

'He said he knew that Carl would be on the riverbank that day so he waited for him then hit him with a piece of wood that he picked up off the ground,' she said. 'He said that I was not to tell anyone what he had done because, if I did, he would kill me as well. I thought about going to my sister's there and then – making a run for it. I'd already got my bag packed.'

'What stopped you?' asked Harris.

'I was frightened at what he would do. I mean, he'd already killed Carl. On the other times when he lost his temper, he calmed down by the morning, so I slept in the spare room and locked the door.'

'And this morning?' asked Harris. 'How was he this morning?'

'Much calmer,' said Anna. 'Like the other times it happened, he said that he was sorry for what he had done. He asked for my forgiveness and begged me not to tell anyone that he had confessed to killing Carl. Then he left the room. I didn't know that he had gone to the pond or that he was going to shoot himself.'

She started to sob and Harris let her cry for a couple of minutes.

'It's a fine act,' he said eventually. The inspector glanced at Gallagher. 'Wouldn't you agree, Sergeant?'

Gallagher nodded his agreement.

'Very well-rehearsed,' he said.

'What do you mean, "well-rehearsed"?' said Anna.

She gave the inspector a dark look, the tears were banished and the vulnerability of moments before had been driven away to be replaced by something much more defensive. Resentful. Challenging the detectives to justify their comments. Harris and Gallagher watched the transformation in startled silence, as did her solicitor.

Harris picked up the documents from the desk.

'Just what I say,' he said. 'It's a fine act.'

'What *are* they?' asked the lawyer.

'This one,' said Harris, sliding the first document across the desk towards her, 'is the reason that we had to take a break. It's a statement from Ronny Carroll, in which he admits murdering Carl Bradby after your client told him that he could go to prison for five years over the snares and that the only solution was killing him. Ronny hopes that if he is honest with us at this stage of the investigation, and confirms that the murder was not his idea but was instigated by your client, the judge will be lenient when it comes to court.'

'No one will believe him!' exclaimed Anna, glaring at him.

'Ordinarily, I might be tempted to agree with you,' said Harris. He slid the printout of Anna's phone calls across the desk. 'But a jury would undoubtedly wish to know why you talked to his brother on several occasions on the days leading up to the murder. Ronny says he was passing on messages about the murder.'

Anna closed her eyes.

'A jury would also want to know about this,' said Harris, placing another piece of paper in front of the lawyer. 'It's an initial report from the Police Scotland pathologist who examined Stuart's body. He says that, in his opinion, the injury to Stuart's stomach is unlikely to have been self-inflicted.'

Anna opened her eyes and watched uneasily as the inspector slid over another document so that Elspeth Cavanagh could read it.

'And this one,' he said, 'is from a ballistics expert attached to the Police Scotland Firearms Unit. As you can see, he believes that Stuart did not kill himself but was shot by someone else and that the scene had been staged. To the best of our knowledge, your client was the only person with her husband at Dark Waters this morning.'

Anna had gone very pale.

'And the final one?' asked the lawyer. She gestured at the remaining document in front of him and spoke in a voice that suggested that she did not really want to know the answer.

'This,' said Harris, sliding it across the desk, 'is from another ballistics expert with the Police Scotland Firearms Unit who says that he is ninety per cent certain that the shotgun that was used to kill Stuart was the same one that was fired at him down by the aviaries, based on the remnant of shells found at the scene. I can't prove it but I think that the earlier threats were nothing to do with your client, maybe they were something to do with another investigation, but I am sure that she took advantage of them to try and shoot her husband with his own gun, assuming that the shells would be too fragmented for us to make the link.'

Anna Liversedge thought for a moment then gave her solicitor a resigned look.

'OK.' She sighed. 'I wish to make a statement.'

Elspeth Cavanagh nodded.

'I don't think you have another option,' she said.

'Let's start with Carl, shall we?' said Gallagher. 'Why did you want him dead? I thought that you said he was exciting? Turned you into a giddy teenager?'

'He did in the early stages of the affair, but he was also a very selfish man, very jealous and a bully,' said Anna. 'When I told him that it was over, he refused to accept it and started threatening me. I did not dare tell Stuart what I had done – you know what he's like when he loses his temper – so I decided to hire someone to kill Carl. Make it all go away. I didn't think I could do it myself.'

'But why on earth go for Ronny Carroll, of all people?' said the sergeant.

Anna gave a slight smile.

'Oddly enough,' she said, 'a woman like me does not have many contract killers in her address book! Ronny was the only man I knew who was capable of doing such a thing and I was pretty sure that there was no way anyone would take him seriously even if he did accuse me. He could not prove what I had said and I knew Davie wouldn't say anything. He said he never talked to the police.'

'You read that wrong,' said Harris.

She gave him a bleak look.

'For what it's worth, I regretted it the moment Ronny killed Carl,' she said.

'And Stuart?' asked Harris. 'Why did you kill him?'

'I had to,' she said. 'Self-preservation. What I told you about last night was true. He did lose his temper. He said he knew that I had been having an affair and he said that he suspected that I'd had Carl killed.'

'What made him think that?' asked Harris.

'I'm not sure but he said it again this morning. I couldn't take the risk of him telling anyone. The rest you know…'

Her voice tailed off and she was silent for a few moments then gave them an odd smile.

'Ironically, it turns out that I did not need Ronny after all,' she said. 'It's actually very easy to kill another human being…'

Epilogue

Seven months later, Harris and Gallagher sat in the public gallery at Carlisle Crown Court and listened to the judge as he sentenced Anna Liversedge to life with a recommendation that she serve at least twenty-five years, after she pleaded guilty to one count of murder and one of conspiracy to murder. The judge described her as a 'calculated and cold-blooded killer'. The week before her sentencing, Ronny Carroll's hope that the judge would reward his honesty with leniency proved ill-founded and he received a life sentence with a minimum of twenty-three years after pleading guilty to the murder of Carl Bradby. Sitting in the public gallery on that occasion as well, Gallagher had murmured 'gotcha!' and he and Harris had surreptitiously shaken hands.

The previous week had seen all the eight members of the AFA who were involved in the attack on the Langdon Estate sent to prison for terms of between eight months and five years, the longest sentences reserved for Guy Robertson and Miriam Coles. The AFA itself had long since collapsed and Dark Waters had also ceased to operate with the rescue centre taken over by the Wildlife Trust which had looked after its birds. 'Think what you will of their methods,' Harris had observed during a conversation with Gallagher, 'the people who violate the environment can breathe a little easier now that Dark Waters aren't watching them.'

The sentencing of Anna Liversedge was the final legal action linked to the series of events that had so occupied the detectives; in Scotland, Jimmy Probert was jailed for ten years for attempted murder and the dumping of chemicals and his brother for seven on the chemicals charge, while Luke McAllister was sent down for eighteen months in acknowledgement of his lesser role in the chemicals operation. Luke's sentence was handed down two days after his grandfather's funeral, the old man having never fully recovered from the injury sustained in the confrontation with his grandson. On the day that Maureen Strothers left the court after the sentencing of the Proberts, with a judge's commendation ringing in her ears, word had filtered through to Levton Bridge that she had been promoted to superintendent. On hearing the news, Jack Harris had smiled but said nothing.

Now, Harris and Gallagher were leaving the court following the sentencing of Anna Liversedge.

'What's your plan for the rest of the day then?' asked Gallagher, glancing at his watch then at his boss. 'We'll be back by half one.'

'Do you know,' said Harris, 'I might do a spot of fishing.'

THE END

List of Characters

Levton Bridge Police:

Superintendent Philip Curtis – divisional commander
Detective Chief Inspector Jack Harris
Detective Inspector Gillian Roberts
Detective Sergeant Matty Gallagher
Detective Constable Alison Butterfield
Detective Constable Alistair Marshall
Detective Constable Sally Orr

Other police officers:

Graham Leckie – intelligence officer with Greater Manchester Police
Detective Chief Inspector Maureen Strothers – Police Scotland
Detective Constable Helen Moore – Police Scotland

Langdon Estate:

Danny Brewster – marketing officer
Janice Garvey – administrative assistant
Miranda Jacobs – office manager

Ronny Carroll – water bailiff
Sebastian de la Roche – owner

Dark Waters – environmental pressure group:

Anna Liversedge – co-founder and joint owner
Stuart Liversedge – co-founder and joint owner, Anna's husband

Anti-Fishing Alliance (AFA) – wildlife pressure group:

Miriam Coles – co-founder
Guy Robertson – co-founder

Other characters:

Carl Bradby – freelance investigator
Elspeth Cavanagh – solicitor
Davie Carroll – Ronny's brother (see Langdon Estate)
Geoffrey Darnell – solicitor
Ross Makin – director of the Three Valleys Wildlife Trust
Gregor McAllister – chairman of Lane End Community Association
Luke McAllister – his grandson
Graham Probert – co-owner of waste disposal company
Jimmy Probert – co-owner of waste disposal company, Graham's brother
Professor James 'Doc' Rokeby – Home Office pathologist

If you enjoyed this book, please let others know by leaving a quick review on Amazon. Also, if you spot anything untoward in the paperback, get in touch. We strive for the best quality and appreciate reader feedback.

editor@thebookfolks.com

www.thebookfolks.com

More books in this series

DEAD HILL (Book 1)

The gruesome murder of a gangland member on a deserted hill brings DI Jack Harris out of his rural reverie. But when the pursuit of the truth sheds light on the detective's own shady past, those around him will question their loyalties.

THE VIXEN'S SCREAM (Book 2)

When a sleepy hillside town is beset by a spate of burglaries followed by a murder, Detective Jack Harris must quickly uncover the link between them. But when the locals become convinced a serial killer is at work, he will find his limited patience stretched to breaking point.

TO DIE ALONE (Book 3)

When a body is found in the woods, Detective Jack Harris is called upon to establish if a murder has taken place. But the victim's connections with a known criminal who has evaded Harris in the past threatens to colour his judgement. Will the detective see the facts for what they are or will his desire to get even turn his colleagues against him?

TO HONOUR THE DEAD (Book 4)

A Pennine town's war memorial is defaced and a WWII veteran is murdered. Are the two events connected, and who would commit such a crime? There is an obvious suspect, but something is not right. DCI Jack Harris must cut through the lies and find the culprit fast.

THOU SHALT KILL (Book 5)

A man is found dead on his allotment. He has been crucified. Who has committed this cruel act? Veteran crime solver Jack Harris and his team must act fast to crack the case and solve the mystery.

ERROR OF JUDGEMENT (Book 6)

A body discovered near a crash site. Dodgy financial dealings. A grieving widow. And someone who'll kill to cover their tracks. DCI Jack Harris reopens a cold case.

THE KILLING LINE (Book 7)

A small rural community is thrown into panic when a local schoolgirl is found dead from a drugs overdose. It is the second in as many weeks. Whilst the locals throw blame on a local rehabilitation centre, detective Jack Harris discovers the girl was murdered. Can he keep the wolves at the door and collar the killer?

KILL SHOT (Book 8)

It is an easy kill for the sniper who takes out a bird watcher protecting the nest of a rare breeding pair. But it's not a straightforward case for DCI Jack Harris. The victim had links to a criminal network, and the detective sees an opportunity to bring them down. But will the mob be too much for this rural detective to cope with?

LAST MAN ALIVE (Book 9)

A man with dementia is missing. Another man has been shot dead in his tent on a hillside. A foreign police force wants the incident hushed up. DCI Jack Harris must join up the dots and get a murderer off his patch even if it means disobeying a direct order.

THE GIRL IN THE MEADOW (Book 10)

When the body of a young woman is discovered under the floorboards of an isolated house during its renovation, questions are raised about DCI Jack Harris's own potential connection to the site. Will he clear his name or will his reputation be forever besmirched in the rural Pennine community?

All FREE with Kindle Unlimited and available in paperback!

John Dean's DCI John Blizzard series

Detective Chief Inspector John Blizzard runs CID in the imaginary northern city of Hafton, England, which is struggling with the lingering effects of years of economic decline.

Being a port, Hafton has more than its fair share of organised crime, and DCI Blizzard fights a running battle against the criminal underbelly of the city.

A no-nonsense detective who speaks his mind, Blizzard's struggles with the politics of the job regularly bring him into conflict with those around him.

All FREE with Kindle Unlimited and available in paperback!

Other titles of interest

COLD CASE ON THE MOOR
by Ric Brady

An unusual spell of hot weather reveals a dark secret on the Yorkshire moors. A woman's body is found in a dried-up reservoir. When the police work out her identity, it brings the past flooding back for ex-detective Henry Ward. He was in charge of the investigation into her disappearance many years ago. Now he is more determined than ever to find her killer.

FREE with Kindle Unlimited and available in paperback!

CRIMINAL JUSTICE
by Ian Robinson

An undercover cop starts walking a thin line when he infiltrates a criminal gang. He sees an opportunity to make some money and take down a pretty nasty felon, but his own boss DCI Klara Winter is on to him. Can he get out of a very sticky situation before his identity and intentions are revealed?

FREE with Kindle Unlimited and available in paperback!

THE BOOK FOLKS

Sign up to our mailing list to find out about new releases and special offers!

www.thebookfolks.com

Printed in Great Britain
by Amazon